The Dreamers

THOMAS H. RADDALL

With an introduction by John Bell

Pottersfield Press

Atlantic Classics Series

Canadian Cataloguing in Publication Data

Raddall, Thomas H., 1903-
  The dreamers

(Atlantic classics)
ISBN 0-919001-32-7

I. Title. II. Series.

PS8535.A44D74 1986   C813   '.54   C86-093845-X
PR9199.3R23D74   1986

Acknowledgements:
"The Dreamers." *Weekend Magazine*, July 30, 1955.
"The Credit Shall Be Yours." *Montreal Standard*, Oct. 16, 1954.
"Brooms For Sale." *Wide Open Windows*. Toronto: Copp Clark, 1947.
"The Drumlin of Joe Tom." *Adventure*, June, 1942.
"Three Wise Men." *Maclean's*, April 1, 1928.
"The Pay-Off at Duncan's." *Blackwood's*, Sept., 1934.
"The Lower Learning." *Blackwood's*, Oct., 1938.
"Mr. Embury's Hat." *Maclean's*, July 1, 1940.
"Swan Dance." *Maclean's*, April 15, 1941.
"The Miracle." *Saturday Evening Post*, Jan. 9, 1943.

Cover painting by Aré Gjesdal, Devil's Island, Eastern Passage, Nova Scotia

Book design: Lesley Choyce
Typesetting: Dal Graphics

Pottersfield Press
RR2, Porters Lake, Nova Scotia
Canada

Published with the assistance of the Nova Scotia
Department of Tourism and Culture

Reprint assistance provided by the Canada Council

Third printing - 1989.

CONTENTS

FOREWORD

At the age of 82, Thomas Head Raddall, a resident of Liverpool, Nova Scotia for 56 years, is rightfully regarded by many readers and critics as one of the Atlantic region's greatest writers. Given his stature, it has naturally been assumed that all of Raddall's major work has by now appeared in book form, much to the regret, it should be noted, of his numerous admirers who have not seen a new work of fiction from his pen since the publication of the novel *Hangman's Beach* twenty years ago.

However, as Raddall himself has demonstrated, time and time again, the exploration of the past can have serendipitous results. This new collection of his short fiction is a case in point.

Not too long ago, some delving into the Raddall Papers deposited at the Dalhousie University Archives in Halifax led to the welcome discovery that over a dozen of the writer's short stories, for various reasons, had not been included in his previous five collections. More importantly, it soon became apparent that the best of the lost pieces, ten in number, were first-rate Raddall. It is these finely crafted tales which constitute the present collection

In terms of their original dates of publication, the stories span nearly three decades in T.H. Raddall's distinguished career. When the earliest, "Three Wise Men," appeared in *Maclean's Magazine* in 1928, he was a young bookkeeper at the MacLeod Pulp and Paper Company in Milton, struggling, in his spare time, to become a short story writer. Twenty-seven years later, when "The Dreamers," Raddall's last story, was published in *Weekend Magazine*, he was an internationally renowned author with many books of fiction and non-fiction to his credit, not to mention two Governor General's Awards.

Such success did not come easily to Raddall. Unaccountably, his second submission to *Maclean's* was rudely rejected, forcing him to spend about two years as a somewhat reluctant contributor to U.S. pulp magazines like *Sea Stories* and *Excitement*. In fact, it wasn't until the spring of 1938, when prompted by regular sales to *Blackwood's*, one of Britain's leading periodicals, and encouragement from the likes of John Buchan (Lord Tweedsmuir), then Canada's Governor General, that Raddall was able to take the plunge and become a professional writer. A year later, twelve of his popular *Blackwood's* stories were collected in *The Pied Piper of Dipper Creek*. In 1942, he published his first novel, *His Majesty's Yankees*, a compelling account of Nova Scotia's response to the American Revolution.

During the two years which followed, Raddall broke into some of North America's most prestigious and lucrative magazines, including *The Saturday Evening Post* and *Collier's*. He also eventually emerged as an accomplished popular historian, writing an award-winning history of Nova Scotia's capital, *Halifax, Warden of the North*, and later, a lively study of the pre-Confederation period, *The Path of Destiny; Canada From the British Conquest to Home Rule: 1763-1850*, for which he received his third Governor General's Award. Although he continued to produce best-selling works of historical fiction, such as *Roger Sudden*, *Pride's Fancy*, and *The Governor's Lady*, he also penned three novels with contemporary settings: *The Nymph and the Lamp*, *Tidefall*, and *The Wings of Night*.

By the time of his much lamented retirement in the early 1970s, Raddall had written more than 20 books, 50 articles, and 70 short stories. His last major work, an autobiography entitled *In My Time; A Memoir*, appeared in 1976. Based on the writer's voluminous diaries, it provides invaluable insight into both the nature of twentieth century Nova Scotia and the development of Canada's literary community since the Depression.

Taken together, his many publications form a body of writing that is equalled by few Canadian authors of his generation, a fact that was recognized in November 1971 when Raddall received the Order of

Canada. Adding to the extent of his achievement has been his steadfast refusal to accept a cent in the way of government grants.

Such fierce independence will come as no surprise, of course, to anyone who has read Raddall. Consciously out of step with modernist literary practices, his writing displays the same virtues as that of his chief mentors: Robert Louis Stevenson, Arthur Conan Doyle, Rudyard Kipling, and Joseph Conrad. As John Buchan observed in his introduction to Raddall's first collection, the Nova Scotian is a natural storyteller who possesses the "rare gift of swift, spare, clean-limbed narrative."

Raddall's fiction is largely centred outside the urban reality which primarily concerned his contemporaries like Morley Callaghan and Hugh MacLennan. Instead, his work tends to focus on past and present life in Nova Scotia's small towns and villages located on the edge of the sea or amidst the vastness of the province's Western forests. Not surprisingly, it is writing rooted in the geography of Raddall's own life since his family's move to Canada from Hythe, Kent in 1913: Halifax, Sable Island, Milton, Liverpool, Kejimukujik, and the North Atlantic.

Drawing on his wide knowledge of Nova Scotian history as well as his early experiences as both a wireless operator in the merchant marine and a white collar worker in frequent contact with the lumbermen, woodsmen, and Indians of Queens County, Raddall set out to interpret his province to the world. Yet for all its particularity of place, there is nothing parochial about his fiction. As the stories which follow unmistakably testify, he has the rare ability to uncover universal truths within the distinctiveness of his own community.

In *The Dreamers*, against the backdrop of an often harsh and unforgiving environment, Raddall celebrates a people who greatly value humour and common sense, a people, moreover, who stubbornly refuse to spurn the past or to bow to adversity. Like the characters which they so vividly portray, these stories will surely endure.

John Bell
Ottawa
April 1986

The Dreamers

The two boys halted on their way down the ridge, standing on a ledge of rock that jutted out of the forest and gave a wide view of the Basin. Far below the water rippled and shone between the long shaggy-wooded hills like a horse-trough made by giants. At the foot of the ridge they could see the buildings of the Habitation ranged about the courtyard with their tall peaked roofs, like a Norman manoir changed from stone to wood and carried mysteriously across the sea, and a little to the left of it the wigwams of the savages.

"When does it come, the Big Canoe?" the Pigeon said.

"Soon," said Biencourt.

"Does it bring plenty of red cloth, and beads, and knives and blankets and all those things?"

"Yes."

"And fire-water to make old Membertou go"—the Pigeon turned his eyes up into his head and rolled his head from side to side. Biencourt grinned.

"I suppose so."

"Will it bring your people more *paskowaage* like this?" the Indian boy pointed to the short gun that Biencourt carried on his shoulder.

"Not many like this," the French boy said. He searched his mind for the Micmac words. "The Big Canoe will bring *paskowaage* like those others you have seen, the ones that fire with a piece of the thong-that-burns. This one that my father brought last year is different. It is rare."

"When are you going to fire this thing?" the Pigeon said. He was itching with curiosity. The other Normanni used guns that fired with a piece of fuse clipped in the cock, and when they went hunting they had to keep a coil of it twined about one wrist with the free end always glowing. This gun of his friend the Normanni boy, the son of the white chief, made its own fire with a little wheel. He had heard of this marvel. He wanted to see it work.

"Soon!" he said discontentedly. "Always you say soon. The Big Canoe comes soon. All spring you have said that. And you will give me a knife soon. The white sagamore, your father, tells your sagamore Membertou that he shall have a red cloak soon, and a hat with a feather to wear when the great ones feast together. Soon, your men say, they will bring Normanni women across the Big Water to live with them, and our women are eager to see these women with white skins. Soon. All soon. You are dreamers, you Normanni. You dream and tell us your dreams."

Biencourt hesitated. His father had cautioned him not to fire the arquebus more than once because the powder supply was low. Until the ship came from France all their supplies were low.

"Look," he said, pointing. "That bird on the branch there — is that a dream?"

"It is a partridge," said the Pigeon impatiently.

"It is a dead partridge," said the French boy. "Watch." He took the gun from his shoulder. The bird was a spruce partridge, one of those stupid creatures that would sit on a branch all day if you made no sudden movement. The gun was loaded with powder and a charge of small shot. He slid aside the cover of the gun-pan and from his powder flask shook a little heap of the precious black grains into the pan. From his pocket he drew the winding key. He fitted it over the little shaft of the lock-wheel and wound up the spring. It made a sound like winding up a watch. The Indian boy regarded all this with enormous interest. Now the French boy adjusted the gun-cock with its important chunk of pyrites at the tip. He put up the gun and aimed. The Pigeon drew away a little and stuffed his forefingers in his ears. These things were marvellous but a little frightening.

The French boy pressed the trigger. The lock-wheel with its rough milled edge like a big steel coin spun sharply against the pyrites. A little shower of sparks. The quick light flare of the powder in the pan. Then a crack like thunder. A spout of white smoke sprang from the muzzle of the gun and seemed to reach almost to the tree where the partridge sat. For some moments the tree was hidden. The sound of the shot went rolling along the hills. Biencourt's shoulder felt numb, but that was not important. The important thing was the smoke drifting off and the partridge making a last dying flutter on the ground.

"Is this now a dream?" said the French boy proudly.

"It is true," the Pigeon said. He added, "Still, one does not know about the other things."

"Those, too, will come to pass," said Biencourt. The Indian boy picked up the dead bird and they went on down the steep hillside in the shadow of the woods. They reached the Indian camp, that stinking place clamorous with children and dogs. The women moved about their tasks. The men squatted in the sunshine playing *al-tes-ta-kun*, tossing the small bone discs on a wooden dish and each time leaning forward eagerly to count the ones that fell with the marked side up.

The Pigeon cried out to them, pointing to the arquebus. "I have seen this *paskowa* make its own fire, *sit-pa-boum*! and kill a bird." He held up the bird for proof and stopped to tell them all about it, with gestures. Biencourt walked on to the Habitation, passing through the gardens laid out and cultivated by the Frenchmen. The Indians would do no work of that sort. It puzzled them to see even the great men of the Normanni, the map-maker, and he-who-laughs-and-talks-always, all laboring at shovel and hoe for hours to prepare this earth for planting. "When the Big Canoe comes," the Indians said, "the Normanni will sit in the sunshine and play *al-tes-ta-kun* like us, and their women will do this grubbing in the earth."

As Biencourt approached the Habitation's massive door he called out to the sentry on the high cannon platform.

"Any sign of the ship?"

"None," the soldier said.

The boy passed into the courtyard where the well stood. It was hot there, shut off from any wind by the four-square arrangement of the buildings, and in the various quarters all the doors and windows stood open for air. He turned into his father's quarters, next to the gate.

The Baron was a big man, sitting now at his table and busy at accounts. He looked up and smiled. The boy was past fifteen and already tall and strong, and dressed like this, with fringed leather leggings to the thigh in the savage fashion, and a leather jerkin, and with his long hair bound in a thong, he looked a part of the country. In another twenty years, the Baron thought, there will be many like him here, able to move freely through the forest, not tied to the coast and dependent always on a ship. He watched the boy clean the new arquebus and stand it in the rack with the worn match-locks which had now served the expedition three hard years. He is like the gun, too, the Baron thought; something new and better than we older ones who belong to another time.

"I think, my son, that you should now go and receive your lesson in navigation. You missed it yesterday."

Biencourt gave his father a comical look. All that boring business with the astrolabe and globes and charts, and those dull, dull mathematics! He walked across the courtyard and entered the quarters of the map-maker. The man sat where Biencourt had seen him most of the winter, at his table with quill and ink and ruler, consulting the heap of notes scrawled on his trips about this coast, putting the result on paper, and decorating the finished charts with little drawings of birds and beasts and fish and Indians. He was shorter than the Baron, with strong hands and quick lively eyes, and yet he was a dreamer like the Baron too. The Pigeon was right, Biencourt thought. They are all dreamers really.

"What are you drawing now?" the boy said. The map-maker looked up and laughed.

"A game. A game in which you put on paper all you know, and then try to guess what you don't. See, here is a rough outline of the coast of this continent so far as it is known, beginning at Panama and ending at Labrador, where all is rock and ice. I have seen part of Labrador. I have been at Panama myself. The continent is very narrow there. If by some miracle one could dig a small canal across it he could shorten the westward voyage to the China Sea by more than fifteen hundred leagues. Now here, far up the coast towards where we are now, the Italian sailor Verrasano and others have said there is another isthmus like the one at Panama. They have described a river in it by which one could go almost to the China Sea. They have even described a wonderful city on that river called Norumbega. Fancies! Wonderful fancies! In these three years in Acadie we have explored every summer towards the south, looking for his river and this Norumbega. We had misfortunes with the savages and with our ships — we were cast ashore in several places — and at last we had to give it up. But I can tell you this. We found nothing but a rough coast with no great river, and from the savages we know that beyond Acadie there is a mass of land stretching for hundreds of leagues. No isthmus. No Norumbega.''

"Then," Biencourt said, "there is no passage towards China in these latitudes?"

"Ah!" The map-maker nodded vigorously. "I believe there is. Somewhere in New France there must be a way to La Chine, and we must find it. When de Monts arrives with new supplies I shall persuade him to seek it further towards the north, not the south."

The boy sat on a bench smiling inwardly. It always worked. If you got the map-maker talking about the road to La Chine he would forget about the navigation lesson he was supposed to give you, he would forget everything. Or if that failed you could get him talking about his three years in Acadie; the first frightful winter at St. Croix, when so many French men perished; and then the move across the great tidal bay and the building of the habitation at Fort Royal here; and the Order of Good Times, the map-maker's own idea, with its formal dress and lively feasts, because to fight the scurvy in the long Acadian winters you had to keep the men cheerful as well as properly fed. Or you could get him talking about his young days as a soldier, fighting in the civil wars, or his adventures with the IX Spaniards in the West Indies and Mexico.

But now there was a cry from outside, in the direction of the gage. The boy and the map-maker leaped up. All about the courtyard they could see heads peering from doors and windows. And now into the courtyard came the Indian chief, that ancient skinny creature who could still see things afar sooner than any of the Normanni.

"*Nabigwon*! he screamed.

"*Nabigwon?*" Biencourt murmured. "Ship!"

He and the map-maker ran up on the cannon platform. The Baron was there already, staring under a hand towards the far end of the Basin where the sea came in between tall cliffs. The sunshine on the water made it difficult to see, and several minutes passed. Then they caught a glint of sunlight on a sail.

"Trumpet!" called the Baron. The Swiss soldier on the platform blew a long blast, but there was no need of it, everybody knew now. They were all running out of the gateway, shouting, laughing, even the five sick men who only a few minutes ago had been lying in their beds. And now the savage camp broke into outcry, and a swarm of Indian men, women and children and dogs came running to join the Normanni at the landing place. After a time old Membertou said doubtfully, "This is not the *nabigwon* that went away. This one is small."

And so it proved to be, a small and weatherbeaten thing with patched brown sails. "This cannot be the Sieur de Monts," said the map-maker. "This is just a fishing barque of St. Malo, of the kind that fish out on the great cod banks each summer and put in to Canseau to dry their catch."

The stranger shortened sail and came up to the anchorage uncertainly. A small boat put off, with two men rowing and another in the stern. When they touched the beach in front of the Habitation the one in the stern leaped out with a slim packet in his hands. He was a young man with a dark sea-toughened face and shrewd black eyes.

"I have a letter for the Baron Poutrincourt," he announced in a Norman accent.

"I am he," said the Baron, holding out his hand for it. "You have supplies for us too, eh?"

"Nothing," said the dark young seaman, regarding the ragged crowd with a mixture of curiosity and contempt. "Oh, there were a few things from the Sieur de Monts, some hams and fruits and sweetmeats, but we ate those on the voyage."

"You dared?" snapped the Baron from his full height.

The Malouin shrugged, flipped his hands and made a mouth. "We ran short of food. Anyhow, we thought you'd all be dead. They tell hard stories in St. Malo of the winters in these parts."

"Come," said the Baron to the map-maker. "And you Lescarbot, and you my son, and you, Captain — what is your name?"

"Chevalier," said the Malouin.

They made their way through the murmur of the crowd. Inside his quarters the Baron shut the heavy door. Outside old Membertou explained to his flock, "It is small, this *nabigwon*. Nevertheless there will be gifts for us, and much food for the Normanni. Tonight we shall feast with them."

Inside, in the hot silence of the narrow chamber, the Baron opened the packet stained with the Malouin's tarry thumbs. The others watched his face as he opened it and began to read, seeing his pleasant features change to a frown and then to something like horror. He read it twice, three times. Then he walked to the window and stood for some minutes with his back towards the others. Nobody spoke. Abruptly he faced about.

"Messieurs, the worst has happened. The letter is from our leader, the Sieur de Monts. All our struggles here have come to nothing. His charter to New France has been cancelled."

"By whom?" cried Lescarbot the lawyer.

"By His Majesty. He has been influenced by our rivals who want the fur trade for themselves."

"But on what excuse?" demanded the lawyer.

The Baron gazed about the room. "You know the religious troubles in France. The Sieur de Monts is a Huguenot. More than half the money our company was Huguenot money. I am a Catholic myself. I think we all are in this room, except perhaps Captain Chevalier."

"I am a Catholic also, m'sieu," said the Malouin carelessly.

"Ah! Well, I had thought with de Monts that we could leave behind those troubles which have torn our country. We thought that here in New France we could work together, Catholic and Huguenot, as Frenchmen together in another world, each keeping his own peace and faith. We knew there would be troubles enough here in this savage country without tearing at each others' throats. And we had trouble enough. That first winter at St. Croix!" He turned to the map-maker. "Do you remember how our priest and the Huguenot pastor quarreled? And how they died together of the scurvy? And how the sailors, those rough fellows, buried them in one grave and said, 'Let them compose their quarrel in the earth' — do you remember that?"

"Yes," said the map-maker.

"A lesson for us all," said the Baron sombrely. "But in France our rivals, those greedy traders who care nothing for religion, have used de Monts' religion as the means of his downfall. That means the downfall of us all here, Catholic and Huguenot, who belong to his company. There are no supplies. We must abandon Port Royal and go back to France. And there is not time to be lost."

Outside the Habitation, beyond the palisade, the silent group in the room could hear the babble of the Indians, and from the courtyard the excited French voices of the workmen and soldiers. No one spoke in the chamber for a long time. Then came the map-maker's voice, calm as always.

"Well, we have proven something here, messieurs. We have proved that Frenchmen can cultivate this soil and raise crops, and we have proved that they can not only survive the winters but live well. That is not lost. It will prove, you will see, a key to New France. For the present we must return to France and think of what we shall do next. Marc, you have a good mind behind that chatter of yours. What do you intend to do?"

"Me?" Lescarbot said, and smiled. "I shall be desolated to go, of course, to leave my garden, my fish pond and my little summer-house that I have built with my own hands. But if I must go, I must, and that's the end of it. But there is something I wish to do, yes. Don't laugh, messieurs. It is to write a book. I don't mean a little volume of bad poetry or a bundle of worse plays — you have seen something of my efforts in that line. My dream is to write and publish a book about this county, this Acadie, the country and its people and the woods and streams and beasts and birds and fish, and to give a history of our adventures here."

"And you, Poutrincourt?" asked the map-maker.

The Baron put his chin out stubbornly. "My future is here — here in Acadie. You know, apart from ourselves, our Frenchmen here are workmen, sailors, soldiers, working for wages, paid by the company. They care nothing for the country itself. When I go out there and tell them they are going back to France they will cheer like madmen. My dream is a true colony here, French men and women and their families, settled here in Acadie and regarding it as their home. This is not the end. Somehow, some time, not far, I shall come back here with my family and with others. Here, you understand, not in some other wild corner of New France. My destiny is here."

He glanced at the boy and saw his son's eyes shining at the prospect. He turned to the map-maker then. "Well," he murmured, smiling now, a little sadly, "We have told our dreams, Marc and I. What's yours — before we go?"

"Before we go — oh, yes. And we must inform the men soon, m'sieu le Baron, and the savages. But before we go, since Marc insists on dreams, I'll tell you mine. It's not like yours. I wish to see French men and women settled in New France, but not merely at Port Royal. You laugh at me, you others, because I'm always talking of the way to China. There must be such a way. But it is not here. We have proved that. The way must be along the great river of Canada, where I sailed with de Monts four years ago. The Indians there drew little maps in the mud and talked about a waterway, a chain of lakes each as big as a sea, all leading on towards the west. Towards La Chine! Such a passage cannot be explored from France, a thousand leagues away. We must first establish habitations like this, not one but many, a cord, a procession along the Saint Lawrence, a population of French people raising their own crops and cattle, depending on themselves." He pointed to the weapon rack across the room. "We must have in New France a population like the Baron's new arquebus, one that makes its own fire. When that is well begun we shall be able to move into the heart of the continent along this wonderful waterway of the savages. And when we can do that, messieurs, we shall find the China Sea. That is my dream."

The boy gazed from face to face. His father had that inspired, almost fanatical look with which he spoke of his faith in Acadie. Marc Lescarbot had the amused, faintly cynical expression that his face assumed whenever the conversation became serious. His mind was in Paris, not here. And the map-maker looked as if he saw exactly what he had described, a new French empire stretching on towards the China Sea. For himself, the boy could think only of Port Royal, the long shining water of the Basin and the wooded hills. Soon I shall come back, he thought, and I shall roam the forest with the wheel-lock arquebus, and with my friend the Pigeon, while the map-maker and his lessons are far away on that absurd road to La Chine.

"Well," the Baron said, "enough of fancies. I must go out now and tell the men and that old withered savage Membertou that we are going away — but that I, I myself, am coming back in another spring. And you, messieurs, had better make your preparations for departure."

He strode out into the courtyard, calling the workmen and soldiers about him. Lescarbot and the map-maker departed towards their quarters. Only the tough young Saint Malo fishing captain remained in the room with the Baron's son. The Malouin pointed at the map-maker's departing back.

"Who is he?" he said curiously. "That fellow with the atrocious Biscayan accent and all the wild talk about La Chine?"

The boy roused himself from the stupor of all this talk and all these fancies. "That," he said carelessly, "is our navigator. Our map-maker. A man of Brouage who's had wonderful adventures and yet dreams of more. His name? His name is Champlain. Samuel Champlain."

The Credit Shall Be Yours

Lieutenant Saxton came out of the officers' quarters and saw his platoon lined up on the gravel of the parade ground. It was a calm morning of Indian summer with a promise of uncomfortable heat after the night's frost. The flag over the fort hung limp in the halliards. A late flock of wild geese flitted across the clear November sky.

The men were standing at ease, but now, seeing Saxton emerge, the sergeant bawled "Ten-shun!" They moved sluggishly, even awkwardly. The eternal labor on the crumbling ramparts of the fort had accustomed them more to ax and shovel than to the manual of arms. The bright scarlet of their coats and breeches had faded long ago to a dingy rust, the stuff itself was threadbare and the torn places had been patched with cloth that did not match. Not one had a whole pair of gaiters or shoes, indeed their shoes had been cobbled and patched so many times that all resemblance to army issue had vanished long ago.

The very Indians in the woods had better footgear. Their black felt hats had faded like their uniforms, with the cocks drawn out of shape by the weather of God knew how many years. Saxton had joined the garrison three summers before with a small draft of recruits from England. His own uniform was still comparatively smart and his freshly pipe-clayed belts and gaiters flashed like snow in the sun. Still, he thought, it wouldn't do for England — not even for a Halifax church parade.

The tired voice of the major was still in is ear. "I'm giving you the best of the men, you understand. Not just to make a good impression on the American troops but, to tell you the truth, because I don't think more than twenty of our fellows could march ten miles and back." That's the measure of us, Saxton thought, twenty men out of eighty capable of a plain day's march. That's what comes to leaving a detachment in a tumbledown fort in the wilderness all this time. Some of them, like that gaunt white-haired sentry on the rampart, had been at Fort Anne nearly forty years. Old Culross, there, had come to the fort from England as a recruit of twenty-four, and there he was still, like Father Time in shabby scarlet, with a musket over his shoulder where the scythe should have been.

The platoon moved off through the main gate and shuffled along the red mud street, past the stores and the handsome painted houses of the merchants and officials, and then the straggling cabins and hovels of the soldiers' families and other common folk. There was a glimpse of Annapolis Basin in which the squat black hulls of the transports sat on the broad glitter towards Goat Island. More than a thousand Acadian men, women and children were crammed into those hulls already, and now the American troops were coming along the valley from Grand Pré like a broom in a gutter, sweeping the last of the doomed population before them.

Lieutenant Saxton set a faster pace. As the soldiers passed the hovels of the *banlieue* their women and a rabble of ragged children ran out, calling to them in a quaint *patois* of English and French. "Where are you going? What is it now?" Lieutenant Saxton snapped "Silence!" over his shoulder, and the sergeant echoed him, "Silence! Silence in the ranks!" as if his own wife were not standing in a doorway with a child in her arms and three more clutching at her skirts, and with those anxious questions on her lips. This is what comes of it, Lieutenant Saxton thought again. All this time in one place. No good. Not soldierly. Thank God I'm as I am. And then, that's smug. Stop thinking like a prig. Stop thinking altogether. The less you think about all this the better.

The last of the cabins fell behind. The street became a narrow wagon-track, deeply rutted, winding around the edge of the river meadows, sometimes crossing a point of woods where the soldiers walked warily, with the sergeant and two or three active young fellows scouting ahead. In such places during its long service in this outpost the company had been ambushed by the Indians more than once. In places where the cart-road wound around the shoulder of a ridge there was a view across the valley, now shimmering in the forenoon heat. The salt flood of Fundy had ebbed out of the river and now in stream ran low between its red mud banks, so that in many places its course could be marked only by the grass-grown dikes of the Acadians. A fitful breeze stirred over the meadows and ran through the tall grass like cloud shadows on a sea. There were clumps of maples by the river and sometimes a lone elm or willow or the brown hump of a haystack left from last year. There were no new stacks. Groups of untended cattle and horses roamed about the meadows and sometimes on a cropped green rise there was a scatter of sheep.

On each side of the valley ran the long walls of the mountains, dark with pine and spruce forest, and in the distance blue and myste- rious in the haze. The winds and rains and frosts of October had stripped the hardwood trees of almost every leaf, although the oaks still clung to their wine-colored foliage and in the small orchards of the Acadians the withered leaves were still falling slowly from the apple trees. At intervals, in a clearing in the edge of the forest, sometimes on a knoll in the meadows, the soldiers passed a small huddle of farm buildings, rude huts and barns of logs and hand-split clapboards for the most part, with the doors and windows shut. The Acadians had closed them carefully when they departed for the ships or slipped away into the woods, as if they were sure of a return. Fowls scratched in the red clay patches between the houses and barns. Pigs foraged in the edge of the woods. The cattle had been turned loose in the meadows. Not a chimney smoked. There was no sign of human life. And yet in the uncanny silence that hung over everything Lieutenant Saxton had an impression of eyes, of a forest full of eyes, watching the passage of his men along the road.

The men sweated in a heat that belonged to August, not November. It was impossible to keep step in the greasy ruts of the road and they did not try. The sound of their march was a slow unending patter. The sergeant and his scouts carried their muskets at the trail, ready for anything. The rest had their weapons slung. Whenever the track passed one of the cold streams running out of the hills Lieutenant Saxton called a halt, and the men threw themselves down and lapped like dogs, and refilled the wooden canteens at their belts.

Three hours passed in this fashion — three hours and eight or nine miles of silence. Then the scouts paused abruptly on a small rise ahead. Saxton saw the sergeant throw up a warning hand. He turned quickly to the platoon. "Ready firelocks!" A hurried unslinging of muskets, the click of pan-steels, the *snick-snack* of hammers coming back. "See to your flints and priming," Saxton said quietly. He flicked his sword out of the worn leather sheath. Indians! A war-party of Canadian *gens des bois*? You never know.

The sergeant and his trio remained in their rigid attitude, more of sombre interest than alarm. As Lieutenant Saxton drew up to them he saw that the rise commanded a long stretch of valley road towards the east, and the whole stretch was crawling with humanity. They moved in ox carts, in horse carts, on horseback and on foot. But mostly they came on foot. The common homespun clothing made the procession a grey stream flowing like the river itself towards invisible Fort Anne. A confusion of voices and the shrill squealing of ungreased wagon-axles drifted on the warm air to the waiting redcoats on the knoll. The soldiers were silent. All this was familiar. They had seen and heard it every day for some weeks now, on every side of the *banlieue*, as they themselves escorted such grey-clad processions down to the town, to the boats and the waiting ships.

A lean old man with white hair fluttering about his shoulders led the rabble, striding along with a staff in his hand like a Moses leading his people out of Egypt. He paused, and so did the others when they saw the still figures waiting in the road where it crossed the rise. There were murmurs of alarm. Then, seeing the familiar faded scarlet of the Fort Anne garrison, they came on again. The old man jerked a horny thumb over his shoulder, crying with a wild face, "*Les Bastonnais!*" Lieutenant Saxton and the sergeant nodded. To the Acadians all the hostile raids and expeditions of a century had come from Boston, hence all American troops were *Bastonnais*. Even the Indians called American soldiers *Bostoonkawaach*, and the name had come to mean something tough and fierce and unrelenting, very different from the easygoing redcoats of Halifax and Fort Anne.

The grey stream went slowly past. The crippled and feeble and the smallest children rode in the wagons. Some of the young women and the older children were perched on scraggy ponies. The rest plodded in the mud. Many of them called out in *patois* to the soldiers as they passed, and the redcoats answered in the same tongue, with shrugs, and with the fluency of long use. At last there was an end. The refugees halted on the road beyond the rise, looking back and wondering what it meant, this rendezvous of the redcoats with *les Bastonnais*.

And now Lieutenant Saxton could see another column approaching, this of men in blue coats and buckskin breeches. The sun gleamed on the muskets slung across their backs. They wore an odd variety of hats and raccoon caps and they walked with the loose and easy stride of men accustomed to such poor tracks through the forest. There was an officer at their head, a tall rugged-featured man in a black cocked hat and with a brave little show of gold lace on his coat. Otherwise there was nothing to distinguish him from his men. His coat was of the same blue, torn and sweat-stained by the fighting at Fort Beausejour and all the labors and the marching since. He wore the same soiled leather breeches, and the same leather knapsack, and carried the same musket as the rest.

Lieutenant Saxton turned to his men. "Ease your hammers and fall out." The soldiers sat or sprawled beside the road, gladly enough. He walked down the road. The American officer snapped a command to his company and they dropped in the long grass and drank from their canteens. The young Englishman put out his hand.

"Lieutenant Saxton, His Majesty's Fortieth Foot," he said formally. The American shook hands with a firm grip. "Captain Leadbetter, the Massachusetts Regiment." He uttered this with a little jerk of his head, with a note of challenge, knowing that his superiority of rank meant nothing to the British regular. His mind still rankled with the scene at Beausejour, where the British commander had gone out of his way to insult the Massachusetts officers, and he was prepared to meet a studied contempt in this precise young prig of His Majesty's Fortieth Foot with a hot contempt of his own.

"I've been sent to meet and guide you to Fort Anne," said Saxton mildly.

"Oh? Well, we've found our own way from Grand Pré this far and I reckon we can manage the rest."

"You seem to have gathered a lot of those people on the way." The American regarded Saxton with a thin smile. "That's what we came for. Have you any objection?"

Lieutentant Saxton hesitated. "Why do you say that?"

Again the thin smile. "You really want to know, Lieutenant? Because I can tell you quick enough. We reckon — us men of the Massachusetts forces — that we've been saddled with your work. We had enough on our hands at Grand Pré and Canard and those places. This business along the Annapolis River was your job of work. Why should we have to march the length of this cursed valley to sweep up what you regulars should have got?"

Lieutenant Saxton flushed and looked away. He was trying to keep his temper. The worst of it was that he could see the American's point.

"Our garrison at Fort Anne is a handful, no more. Eighty rank and file, some of them old men and invalids. Nevertheless," he added stiffly, "we have been able to persuade and move about a thousand people to the ships."

"Persuade!"

"We were in no position to use force — we few."

"Three men and a boy with muskets can use force if they've a mind to it," Leadbetter snapped. "And we've a mind to it. That's the difference. My men would kill those people at the drop of a word. They hate a Cajun like the plague. For that matter so do I."

"May I ask why?"

"I could give you a lot of reasons, but one will do. I was one of Colonel Nobel's men at Grand Pré in the winter of Forty-seven."

"Oh?" Lieutenant Saxton raised his eyebrows. "That was before my time here. But I've heard of it, of course. And it seems to me that Noble's men were attacked by a war party of French rangers and Indians from Canada. The Grand Pré people had nothing to do with that."

The American spat the straw from his mouth. "They had everything to do with it," he said with a cold violence. "There we were billeted in the Grand Pré houses. A stormy winter night. The Cajuns of Grand Pré betrayed our presence to Coulon de Villiers in the first place, and in the second place they guided his rangers and Injuns from house to house there in the snow and the dark. Colonel Noble was dragged from his bed and murdered in his shirt. I saw five of my men, one my own brother, stabbed and shot and tomahawked the same way. So I know what I'm talking about. Well, we had to wait eight years but now we've paid out the Grand Pré people in some measure for all that. When they were crying and lamenting on their way down to the boats I tell you I could hear nothing but the cries of my men there that winter night."

Lieutenant Saxton was silent. There was no answer to that. But he was still ruffled at the American's attitude.

"Why do you suggest that we — the garrison at Fort Anne —haven't done our duty?" Captain Leadbetter regarded him. Then, with a sardonic grin he gestured towards a log at the roadside. "Suppose we sit a minute. We'll have to march again right soon if we're to make Fort Anne by dark." They sat, and Captain Leadbetter pulled another stalk of grass and put it between his teeth.

"I confess," he said casually, "I've been hankering to say this to some officer of yours. You Englishmen, you people at Fort Anne, you've been in this country nigh on forty years, or the garrison has. That's a sight of time."

"Yes," Lieutenant Saxton said.

"Well, there you are, His Majesty's Fortieth Foot, or a company of it anyhow, living in the midst of the Cajun people all this time. What's happened? You know as well as I do. Your commandant and half your officers and men are married to Cajun women, their children speak French as good or better than English, and all those younkers have been baptised by a Romish priest. That's so, isn't it?"

"True," Lieutenant Saxton murmured. "You must understand that there's been no English chaplain at Fort Anne for many years. The women wished to have their children baptised — that was natural, surely? — and there was Father des Enclaves, a very good old man who has been a friend to English and French alike..."

"Ha! So you say. Well, anyhow, there you are, mixed up with the Cajuns right and left, and what's the consequence? Do you deny that your own major — what's his name, Handfield? — and several other of your officials at Fort Anne are all married to daughters of one Madame Winniett? And isn't it true that this Madame Winniett, this Cajun woman, sits at all the fort councils and has her say? That's what we hear. We hear she practically runs the fort and town. So when the order comes to gather up all the Cajuns and ship 'em off, you redcoats are in the deuce of a stew, what with your Cajun wives and sweethearts, and all their brothers and sisters and uncles and aunts and what not scattered up and down the Annapolis River. So what does your Major Handfield do? Nothing! He got his orders in July and he didn't do a damned thing till this month, when he got a rap on the knuckles from Halifax and had to make a stir. So then he sends his men out, and he *persuades* — that's your word and I daresay it's the right one — he persuades about a thousand of these Cajuns that they might as well come in and go aboard the ships. At the same time he makes it clear, by his own neglect, that if the rest want to skip into the woods and wait till the whole thing's blown over, why, he can't stop 'em. That's true, too, isn't it? So that's where we come in — us blue-coats, us Americans that know our duty when we see it, us men of the Massachusetts Regiment that the governor down to Halifax knows he can rely on. We get our orders and here we are." Captain Leadbetter gazed up the road with an angry satisfaction. "We've picked up two or three hundred of your Cajun friends, and I reckon we'll nab as many more by the time we reach the fort. I've got flanking parties working through the woods each side of the valley, flushing 'em out like partridges. See there." He pointed. A thick column of smoke was rising far across the meadows. "We've fired every house and barn as we came along."

Lieutenant Saxton swallowed. "That seems a needless waste."

"It's commonsense. Thanks to your major's shilly-shallying a lot of young Cajun men have escaped into the hills and joined the Indians, and there they are, with guns in their hands and powder to burn. My men have been fired on a dozen times between Grand Pré and here. Do you think we'd leave a scrap of shelter for 'em now? Let 'em shiver through a winter in the forest and next springtime you'll see 'em coming in like lambs — you and your Major Handfield. You can persuade 'em then. You're good at that."

Captain Leadbetter got to his feet. "I guess we'd better move along. I suppose you'll want to lead the march — you regulars?"

"For the look of things, yes," Lieutenant Saxton said. "My commandant will expect that."

"The credit shall be yours," said the American in his bitter voice. Lieutenant Saxton shrugged and walked up the road. "Fall in," he said.

The long procession began to move through the meadows in its tri-colored sections, like a long grey snake with a scarlet head and an ominous blue tail. The familiar sounds arose again and seemed to hang in the hot air, the murmur of men and women and children, the shouts of teamsters, the jolt of wheels, the piercing protest of wagon-axles, the click and rattle of muskets and accoutrements, the patter and plod of feet. But somehow Lieutenant Saxton could hear nothing but the American's last words, like a chant going on and on through distance and through time.

Brooms for Sale

This is a true story which happened many years ago. Greta was a young widow then, with a boy aged nine. They lived on a small farm in the woods west of the La Have River, near the coast of Nova Scotia. They were very poor.

Greta did all the farm work herself, tending the cattle, ploughing, seeding, and harvesting. In winter she got her own firewood with an axe in the woods. She was a tall Nova Scotia girl with the heart of a man. She had not the strength of a man, though, and no men lived near enough to help her. That was why the house and barn needed repair, and the fences were falling down. That was why each year the crops were smaller. But Greta would not give up.

One winter she thought of a way to get some extra money. There was a fishing village towards the mouth of the La Have, not many miles away. When the fishermen fitted out their vessels each spring, they needed all sorts of things. One thing was a supply of good brooms—but not the kind you buy in the shops. Fishermen must have a very stiff and strong broom, to sweep the deck after cutting and cleaning the day's catch.

Greta had grown up in a shore village and had seen such things made. You take a stick of birch wood about four feet long and three or four inches thick. Then you take a good sharp jack-knife. First, you must remove the birch bark. Then you start at one end of the stick, cutting a splint or shaving about half an inch wide and about as thick as the knife blade. You keep pushing the knife blade to within eight inches of the other end. There you stop. You go back and start another splint. You keep doing that, round and round the stick, until it is no more than an inch and a half thick. And there is your broom handle.

Now you take the bush of splints hanging near the other end, and bend them back over the eight inches of solid wood remaining there. You bind them together tightly in that position with strong cod-line, and with an axe you cut them off at about twelve inches below the cord. And there is your broom, all in one piece.

The Bank Fleet was very large in those days, and in the course of a season each vessel used a number of brooms. So each winter the outfitters bought a good supply.

Greta decided to make some brooms. The days were short and there were many chores to do in the house and barn, not to mention the wood-pile. She would have to do this extra chore after dark. The whittling made such a mess in her clean kitchen that she took part of the barn for a workshop.

Every evening after supper, when the little boy was asleep, she went to the barn, lit a fire in a rusty tin stove, and sat there hour after hour cutting splints by the light of a lantern. Her hands were used to hard work but after a time the grip on the knife made them sore. She tried wearing gloves, but that was awkward. So she tied a strip of linen over the blisters and went on. What pain she suffered, you can guess. But at last her palms were rough and hard, and she could work without a bandage. Sometimes she made four or five brooms before midnight.

By the end of January she had two hundred and forty brooms. It was time to sell them.

One chilly morning in February, she hitched the mare Judy to the sleigh, loaded her brooms, helped her child into the seat, and started for West La Have. She left the little boy in the care of her nearest neighbours, three miles down the road. It was pleasant driving through the woods, with the runners creaking on the snow and the harness bells ringing.

The village appeared, with its wharves and stores, and the wide frozen surface of the river. Greta got out of the sleigh happily. But in the first store she had disappointing news. The ship outfitters at West La Have had a full stock of brooms. They could buy no more.

"You might sell them down the river at East La Have," a store-keeper said, pointing over the ice. Greta looked. In the clear winter air the river did not seem very wide—half a mile, say. And three miles down the east shore was a chance to sell her precious brooms.

"The ice is good," the man said. "Several teams have been across to-day."

So Greta headed the mare across the river. It was pretty, she said afterwards—ice on the broad stream as far as you could see; the white banks and the dark woods; and blue smoke rising in small wisps from the houses by the shore.

When she reached East La Have she was stiff from her long drive in the cold, but she entered the store with a quick step and an eager face. The store-keeper looked out at her load and shook his head.

"Sorry, lady, but it seems everybody's been making brooms this winter. We've got too many now."

Half a dozen fishing captains sat by the stove, smoking and talking over the coming season on the Banks. They looked at the woman from up the river. Her coat was cheap and old, too thin for this sort of weather. They saw the worn overshoes, the home-knit woollen cap, the hands twisting anxiously inside the grey mittens. They looked at her tight mouth, and her eyes holding back the tears.

One of them said quietly, "Buy her brooms. If you don't, we will." The store-keeper called one of his clerks to carry the brooms inside. They made a great heap on the floor.

"Let's see, now. Two hundred and forty brooms at twenty-five cents ..."

"Forty cents," the fishing captain said. "Those are good brooms. I'd say you made them yourself, didn't you, ma'am?"

"Yes," Greta said.

The store-keeper counted out ninety-six dollars—nine tens, a five, and a one. Greta thanked him and the captains in a small, choked voice. As she went out the door one of them said. "You'd better drive home smart, ma'am. Looks like snow." She noticed then that the sunshine was gone, the sky was filled with a grey scud coming in very fast from the sea. A bleak, uneasy wind was blowing this way and that.

Greta had no purse. She stopped and fastened the bank notes to the inside hem of her skirt, using a big safety pin. She drove off, humming a tune to herself, and thinking of the things she could buy now for her boy and for the farm. Before she had gone far, the snow began to fly in small hard specks. When she reached the crossing place, a blizzard was blowing. She could not see across the river.

She turned off the road onto the ice, following the faint tracks of the other teams. After ten minutes the old tracks disappeared, buried in the new snow sweeping along the ice. She had to trust the horse to find the way. Greta was not afraid. After all, it was only half a mile or so.

The snow was now so thick that she could not see past Judy's ears. She let the reins go slack and crouched down in the seat, trying to find a little comfort in the storm. There was none. The snow whirled and stung; it seemed to come from every side. Sometimes it stopped her breath, like a cold white cloth laid over her mouth and nose. The little mare kept plunging her head and snorting in the blasts.

The way seemed strangely long. Greta noticed that the light was growing dim. The afternoon had gone. Soon now, surely, she must see the west shore looming through the storm. The horse went on and on, slipping here and there on patches of bare ice.

At last Judy came to a stop. Greta peered into the swirling snow and saw a dim, pale shape ahead. She shielded her eyes with her mittened hand for a better look. Through the snow-gusts she could see the thing was large, with three slim objects standing upon it and reaching up into the murk. Trees, of course! She cried thankfully, "Good girl, Judy! There's the shore. I knew you'd find it!"

She urged the horse on with a jerk at the reins. Judy went on a few steps and stopped again. The object stretched right across her path. It was close and clear now, and Greta gasped. Her very heart seemed to stop beating. For there, like a ghost risen out of the ice, lay a ship. A ship, of all things! A big schooner with three tall masts, all crusted with snow. What was it doing there? Slowly her mind filled with an awful suspicion. She tried to put it aside, but it came back. At last she faced the truth.

The little mare had been lost all this time. Instead of crossing the ice, they had been wandering down the river, towards the open sea. They were now somewhere near the mouth, where the ice was never safe. To prove it, here was the big three-master, frozen in where the crew had left it moored for the winter.

Poor Greta's heart was beating again in slow hard thumps. She was frightened. She did not know which way to turn. Were vessels anchored with their bows upstream or down? Or were they just moored any way at all? She could not remember.

It was quite dark now. Greta's arms and legs felt numb. One thing was certain, she was freezing there in the bitter wind and snow. So was the little horse. They must move or perish. Greta made up her mind. She got down and took hold of Judy's bridle, turned the sleigh carefully, and began to walk, leading the horse straight away from the long, pointing bow-sprit of the schooner.

The strongest blasts of the storm seemed to come from the right. Greta kept the wind on her right cheek. In that way at least she would avoid moving in a circle.

"Suppose the wind changes?" asked a small cold voice inside her. But that was the voice of fear, and she refused to listen.

The effort of walking took some of the cold ache out of her legs, but there was no feeling in her hands and feet, and her cheeks felt like wood. She kept changing her hold on Judy's bridle and rubbing her face with the other hand. The storm tore at her long full skirs and darted icy fingers through her thin coat. The world seemed full of snow, driving in a sharp slant on the wind, and sweeping along the ice with a hiss like escaping steam.

The mare was not shod for this sort of footing. She slipped and stumbled and seemed very tired. And Greta herself felt weary and empty. She had eaten nothing since the hasty breakfast at the farm. Sometimes the wind lulled, and the cloud of fine snow drifted slowly about them. Its touch then was soft upon the cheek. Greta was tempted to let Judy go, to lie down on the ice and let that cold white power go on brushing her face and soothing her fears and worries. Somehow the snow made her think of bed-sheets, clean and cool to the skin. How nice it would be, just to lie down and sleep away the night!

But whenever Greta's eyes closed, and the strength seemed to flow out of her limbs, there came into her mind a picture of the lonely boy at the neighbours' house, with his nose against the glass. She opened her eyes then, and stepped forward strongly in the darkness.

As the night went on, this happened many times. Greta became more and more drowsy with the cold, and more weary, and the little horse lagged and stumbled worse and worse. Finally, after one of those dreamy pauses, as Greta began to lead the horse again, she came upon a black patch in the ice ahead. It extended to the right and left as far as she could see. She moved closer—and stepped back in alarm. It was water—open water. She could hear it lapping against the edge of the ice.

She thought, "This is the end. We have come to the sea."

She closed her eyes, praying slowly and silently. She stood there a long time. At last she put her chin up. Aloud she said, "Judy, it's all or nothing now. Suppose it isn't the sea—suppose it's just the flooded ice along the shore! You know, where the ice sinks and buckles when the tide falls down the river. There's only one way to prove it, Judy. I must go to the edge and let my feet down into the water. Come, girl! Steady now! Come!"

Greta led the mare to the edge of the ice. The water looked very black. The snow was blowing harder than ever.

"If only I could see," she thought, "just for a minute. Just for a second. If only I could be sure." But there was only one way to be sure in this stormy blackness. She took at turn of the reins about her wrist, stooped, and lowered her left foot into the water. It came to her ankle, to her knee. The cold grip of the water sent a pain to her very bones. She gasped and lost her balance.

For one wild moment Greta thought she was gone. The sea! She was plunging into the sea! But her feet came upon something now, something slippery but solid. It was the sunken ice. She was standing over her knees in water. She paused to gather courage and her breath. She waded out to the length of the reins. The flooded ice held firm. It was tilted against hidden rocks, and now the water barely reached her trembling knees.

"Come, Judy," she cried, and pulled on the reins. The mare snorted and would not more. Greta threw her whole weight on the reins. Judy tried to draw back, but her worn iron shoes had no grip on the ice. Snorting with fear, she was dragged over the edge into the water. Greta found herself being dragged by the reins about her hand.

The horse had floundered past her. She caught hold on the lurching sleigh. Dimly she saw a solid whiteness looming out of the windy dark. It was the shore—a pasture deep in snow.

Greta took the mare's head and led her up the bank. There was a low fence. The poles were rotten and she broke them down. She led Judy along inside the fence, wading through the drifts until she came to a gate and saw a light. Then she was standing at Judy's head outside a house and crying for help.

A man and a woman came to the door. She cried again, and they ran out to her. The man unhitched Judy quickly and took her off to the warmth and shelter of his barn. The woman half-led, half-carried Greta into her kitchen. Greta's clothes were crusted with snow, her wet skirts frozen stiff. But before she would let the good woman do anything for her, she stooped and turned up the icy hem of her skirt.

The precious packet was still there. She counted the notes with her numb white fingers. She laughed shakily. It was all there, the money she had made with her own hands, the money she had saved by her own courage in the storm.

The Drumlin
of Joe Tom

In our province there is scarcely a brook where you can't pan a trace of gold, if you work at it. A queer thing, that, in a region where no man makes easy living, and since it was first discovered men have sunk their savings and their sweat in holes all over the countryside, in hopes of fortune. Here and there in the bush you find the gray heaps of tailings, the rotten and collapsed shaft-timbers, the red-rusted boilers and scrap, the scattered bricks and crazy wooden ruins of small crushers, or maybe on the foundation stones of the buildings and huckleberry bushes sprouting in the red mould that once was beams and planks and boards; and you say what fools men are. Fools, maybe. But gold is there. That is the devil of it, the grinning, teasing, beckoning, blood-squeezing, sweat-drinking devil of it. Pray with me that Satan, who blew these thin veins of ore into our bedrock in the first place, will suck them all back into the hot maw of the earth, out of sight and mind. I am thinking of Joe Tom's gold mine.

It is strange to me, an old man who has for fifty-five years lived the nomad life of a Methodist minister, who has lived the past thirty on the shores of the Pacific, a continent's width from home—it is strange to come back and find myself a Rip van Winkle, seeing new faces, new homes, new roads, new this and that in the old scenes, to find myself unknown; and yet to hear the country folk talking of gold, of a mother lode, of an Eldorado hidden in what is still the wilderness of western Nova Scotia; to find the legend of Joe Tom's mine widely spread and firmly held—and to realize that I alone know the truth—the secret, if you like.

Let me begin at the beginning, my own beginning in the little white farmhouse looking out upon Fairy Lake. That was in 1861, when old men lived who were the pioneers of that inland district. I have sat on the knee of a man who was in the *Shannon's* foretop when she fought the *Chesapeake*. Does that sound incredible? My grandfather was the John Devonshire who first ventured up the river from the coast, and cut out a farm in the lake country amongst the Indians.

He got along well with them, perhaps because he had to; at any rate he learned their life and language, and afterwards, when the settlements came and spread, he was the Indians' friend and counsellor in all their dealings with the whites. My father inherited those responsibilities, and I well remember the lean proud men, the silent brown women, the famished bright eyes of the children, drifting into our big kitchen when the times were hard and my mother feeding them beans, and corned beef and pork, and bread and molasses and such-like. I remember how much those brown people ate, and the way they went off without thanks, without words of any sort; and how they brought gifts of moose and caribou meat whenever their hunting was fortunate, and bear hams for smoking, and sacks of wild duck and geese and partridge which they dumped in a cloud of feathers on the kitchen floor, and withes strung with fat trout. They sometimes brought furs, which my father would never accept. So they traded the furs in New Kerry settlement for odds and ends of clothing, and bright trash for their women, and powder and shot for their old guns, and for rum. Mostly for rum, I'm afraid.

They lived in little gipsy groups, wintering in the lake country near the farms, and moving down the rivers to the coast for the spring run of smelt, and the kiack run, the salmon run, and the easy life by the clam flats. In fall they appeared again, mysteriously, amongst the bright leaves of the hardwoods by the lakeside, and patched up their old bark wigwams for winter, and gathered dead limbs for fuel, piling them tent-fashion to keep them dry and clear of the snow. They buried their occasional dead in an ancient cemetery of their people across the big lake, scratching shallow graves in the gravel under the tall red pines, and to keep off intruders told how the lake was haunted by little spirits. The Scotch, and the English like my grandfather, laughed at those tales, though they respected the brown men's graves. But the New Kerry folk believed in leprechauns and such-like themselves, and called the place Fairy Lake.

Ten years before I was born, an Australian miner went home from the California diggings and found gold on his own farm, and started the great Australian rush. That set people all over the world scratching in their own back yards, the Bluenoses with the rest. Gold was found all over the Atlantic slope of our peninsula, in wandering meager veins that seldom paid to mine; promises that went on and on with no fulfillment. Where the veins crossed was often a pocket of nuggets and dust, a swelling of rich ore, just enough to whet the appetite for more, for another rummage in the bush, another stripping of the vein, another shaft, another stope, another pouring of money and sweat into the hole in the ground.

One day—it must have been in '71, for I was about ten—Joe Tom walked into our house to see father. This Joe Tom was a fine Indian. With the Maltee boys and some others he had given up the wandering habit of his people and cleared a bit of land by the shore of Fairy Lake, not far from ours. He built a small log house, and a barn of long slabs from the sawmill at Jock's Landing, and kept a pair of work-oxen and a cow and some hens and pigs and a woman named Lizzie. They were childless, and Lizzie had adopted a half-breed child, fruit of a lumberman's fancy for an Indian woman up the lake, a little dark girl-thing they called Molly. Joe Tom was a good farmer as Indians go, but now and again the old free life caught hold and dragged him off into the bush alone for weeks on end. He knew the wilderness of lakes and forest in the western thumb of our province as you know the lines of your palm, and whenever Judge Carron came to hunt and fish he hired Joe Tom for guide.

I was in the parlor when Joe Tom came, busy at my schoolbooks, and he looked at me and then at my father, and said, "Demsher, I want talk by myself."

Father gave me a glance. "Never mind the boy, Joe Tom. What are you making mystery about?"

Joe Tom had never acted like that before. He was about fifty then, a tall man in a red shirt, a pair of linsey-woolsey trousers all patched with different cloth and moccasins of moose-hide; and a black mane of hair swept his shoulders. He pulled a small caribou-skin pouch from the breast of his shirt and from it poured a little heap into father's hand.

"What's this?" my father said.

"*Wis-ow-soo-le-awa*," answered Joe Tom, looking at me. That is the Micmac for gold, and he thought I wouldn't understand; but I did. What I don't understand, even now, is how Joe Tom knew it was the stuff the white men talked about. Nobody in our part of the country had ever seen gold in the raw. But the Indians' fancy had long been caught by the talk, by the notion of something valuable lying about the woods, in the rocks and streams, that would buy all the things they'd never been able to buy, and all so simple—finders, keepers, like a legacy from the old splendid gods, and waiting all this time.

"Are you sure?" my father said, staring in his hand.

"Yuh."

"Then you'd better not tell anybody else, Joe Tom."

"Yuh."

"Is there more where this came from?"

"Some."

"A lot, Joe Tom?"

"Some."

Father poured the stuff back carefully, and Joe Tom put away the pouch in his shirt. He said no more; but it was as if he asked a question, and father knew, and was pondering the answer. My father walked over and fiddled with the big glass lamp on the parlor table, and then to the mantel, straightening china dogs and vases, and the daguerrotype of himself and mother taken in Milltown; then he pushed his hands deep in his trouser pockets and rubbed his chin against his shoulder as if his beard itched, and stared at me under his brows, and I put my eyes down to my book, for he looked very stern.

I know now what he was thinking, He was thinking there would be a flocking of miners and speculators and rum-sellers and other outlandish people into our quiet district if the news got around, and he hated it. That had happened already, in many places in the province.

"The sensible thing, I suppose," he said slowly, "is to show me, or Judge Carron, next time he comes from Annapolis, or somebody else you can trust, where the stuff is. Have the land measured off and staked. Then get the government to proclaim this region a mining district, and file your claim. Then nobody can take it from you, Joe Tom."

The Indian shook his head solemnly and looked past father's shoulder. "Is bad luck, Demsher. Is bad luck show white people where is money."

I think that hurt father a bit. The Indians had always set us Devonshires a little apart from the rest of the whites. Stiffly, he said, "Then bring out the stuff, a little at a time, and I'll get Judge Carron to sell it for you. That way, no one'll suspect where it comes from. If you take that stuff into Milltown there'll be an uproar clean to Cape North." He was silent a moment; then he burst out, "I wish to God you'd never found it, Joe Tom!"

Then began the queer transactions that went on, year after year, till the summer of '81. At intervals Joe Tom would vanish into the wilderness; and after a time, never less than a fortnight, he would sidle into our house with the little heavy pouch, looking mighty sly. Father was in the habit of sending Judge Carron a firkin of butter from time to time, and it was a simple matter to put the packet of gold in the top and nail on the head. Our bank was in the country town, down the river. Judge Carron lived at Annapolis, on the other side of the province. He took Joe Tom's gold to the bank there, and after a time the cash came by mail in the coach to Duncan's Corner, and my father passed it to Joe Tom. It might have gone on indefinitely but for two things.

One was that Joe Tom began to spend money. He started with a fine horse from Paddy Monahan, the New Kerry horse trader, and a fancy riding-wagon from the carriage factory in Milltown. Then he got a silver-mounted harness from somewhere. On fine Sundays he used to drive to Mass at New Kerry, then on to Duncan's, with a plug hat down to his ears and a claw-hammer coat over his red shirt, and

Lizzie beside him in her beaded squaw-cap and a black bombazine dress all sewn with brilliants and spangles; and Molly in the seat behind, in a white-girl's outfit that made you realize she was growing up, and mighty pretty, too. That was a sight to behold.

He bought a dozen chiming clocks and set them on shelves about his shabby hut; they never kept quite the same time, and about the quarter and the hour you would hear clocks striking in succession all over the house. He got an American organ, and until she grew bored with it, the girl Molly used to sit at the thing for an hour at a time, pedalling furiously and running her brown fingers up and down the keys. He fitted out Lizzie and the girl with all kinds of gaudy jewelry, and never wore less than three watches and chains himself; and up in New Kerry he used to buy rum. He was canny about that, and would never drink in company, knowing well how *buk-ta-wich-ke* loosened the tongue. He took the stuff home and drank alone, and lay about the shack in a stupor for days at a time.

Father raged, but he couldn't do anything about it. If he quit handling the gold for Joe Tom, the Indian would take it to someone else, and the real turmoil would begin.

The second thing was that Lizzie died in '79, and Joe Tom and Molly went to Father O'Hearne in New Kerry and were married. That caused some talk amongst the women on the farms. Joe Tom was nearing sixty, though you mightn't have guessed it from his looks. The girl was only seventeen, with enough white in her blood to give her a fine-drawn look and a figure. But she took marriage with Joe Tom as a matter of course, apparently, and after some thought people said it was just as well. She was too pretty to be running around loose. They remembered how she came to be born. But things weren't quite as simple as all that. Four or five months after the marriage, Molly had a baby—a baby as white as you or me, and everybody knew it was Jim Ingleson's.

This Jim Ingleson was a worthless sort, about twenty-six with curly yellow hair and bloodshot blue eyes and a weak wet mouth. He'd deserted a vessel loading lumber at Milltown a few years before. I fancy his captain was glad to see the last of him; but Jim walked the road through the woods to Duncan's Corner to make sure—forty miles, about as far as you can get from the sea in Nova Scotia—and begged and loafed from one farm to another. When the Corner got tired of him, he drifted on to the Irish at New Kerry, and from there by a natural law of gravity to the Indians at Fairy Lake. He had been around our part of the country for two years when Joe Tom's Molly gave birth to the white child. He was living then with the Maltees, a Micmac family who had a shack just a mile or two the other side of Joe Tom's.

All this was sorry enough. But now we heard rumors of Joe Tom's gold, and knew that poor easy Molly had talked as well as loved too much. The tale ran like a fire in grass. The old Indian's affluence had puzzled the countryside for years. Here was the answer, and every second man in the district was scouring stream-beds and chipping boulders and keeping an eye on Joe Tom.

About that time I went away to college. I'd done well in the country schools, and my mother was set on my going into the ministry. In those times every mother's ambition was to have a minister in the family—and there are worse, it seems to me. Anyhow, I didn't meet Joe Tom again till the next summer holidays. That meeting I shall never forget.

It was July and thunder weather, with nothing stirring, not even the locusts. Woolly clouds piled in high mountains in the sky, gray at the edges and blue in the distance, hung over the lake and the fields and the woods, and seemed to shut in the heat like the top of an oven. We sat on the stoop, gasping, and waiting for the rain. It came about two o'clock in the afternoon. The thunder, after grumbling around all morning, came to a head with a crash, and a great splatter of lightning ripped down the sky, very bright against the darkness beyond the lake. Then we saw the rain coming in a dark line across the water, kicking up little red splashes in the dust of the road, then pattering, then drumming on the dry roof shingles. We couldn't see the lake for the downfall, and the road at the foot of our fields shone red like the wet clay of Fundy at low tide, and water chuckled down the gutter-spouts into the puncheons where mother caught washing water, and our ears were full of a great hiss, like all the steam in the world. Overhead the storm rattled and boomed, and father kept looking up at the lightning rods on the barn.

Suddenly there was a figure on the road. All the farms in our lake district sit on hillocks of deep soil—what geologists call drumlins—with swamps and woods between, like small cropped islands rising out of the forest.

This figure came out of the woods from the west, a tall man, stooped, and running hard with short quick steps, toes in, the Indian way. As he turned in at our gate and came splashing up the steep lane that joined us to the lake road and the world, we saw it was Joe Tom. His mouth hung open, showing the black stumps of his old teeth, and the cords of his lean throat were like hard taut wires, and his dark eyes bulged as if pushed from within. We came to our feet in a hurry and ran out into the rain, crying out to know the matter, and as we came together in the downpour Joe Tom threw himself at my father's feet, gasping and choking and uttering little snatches of words that made no sense in English or Micmac. Father tried to get him on his feet, but he clung there to father's trouser legs, in the red mud of the lane.

"Demsher," gasped Joe Tom at last. "I killed a man. I killed Ingleson. Save me! Save me!" His voice rose to a scream on those last words, and you would have to know Indians to know the horror that filled Joe Tom.

The Indians had a great awe of the law. One or two had wandered into the county courthouse during spring or fall sessions, and came away with solemn tales. The notion of being dragged into that echoing place, to be stared at from all sides by white men in Sunday clothes, to be droned over by strangers in black gowns, with hands full of mysterious papers, to be faced day after day by that other stranger on the high dais, with his black gown, his immaculate white stock, and his face of an old tired eagle; and at the last to be taken out to the jail yard, with a rope about your neck, and hauled up to a beam and left to kick your life out—this was a horror that haunted the Indian folk. I suppose the whites had rubbed in the details pretty carefully, for their own sake, in the early days. So Joe Tom, who had never feared the death that waits in so many forms for woods folk, now lay in the pelting rain and begged my father for his life.

It was my mother who got Joe Tom indoors. She appeared quietly beside us and stooped, and put a hand on his shoulder. "Get up, Joe Tom!" she commanded sharply. "The idea—getting yourself all wet, at your age. Come into the house and stop all this nonsense."

We left him slumped in the old barrel chair in the kitchen, dripping water on the floor and watching mother as she went about her work, with the eyes of a terrified dog. Father and I hitched old Darby to the buggy and whipped his surprised hide all the way to Joe

Tom's. We found Molly in a rocking chair by the stove, rocking, rocking, rocking, with a face like white stone, and the child clasping in her arms.

Jim Ingleson was stretched on the floor, staring with dead fish-eyes at the rough board ceiling. The top of his head near the brow was hollow where it should have been round, and blood still oozed slowly through his soiled yellow curls, though his heart was as dead as his eyes. In the woodbox behind the stove stood an old muzzle-loader that belonged to the Maltee boys, the stock bound with brass wire to hold an old split in the wood. Father sniffed the muzzle. It hadn't been fired, not recently anyway. He thrust the ramrod down the barrel and found it loaded, but there was no cap on the nipple. The butt had been whittled in a deep half-moon for the shoulder, the way the Indians liked a butt to fit, and one of those sharp wooden horns was plastered with blood and hair.

The roof of the shack leaked in several places, and the drip-drip, loud in the awful silence, set my teeth on edge; but suddenly all the clocks began to chime, one after another, and the child howled.

There were two magistrates in the district. One was Mr. Craig at Duncan's Corner, a just man but rigid, a stern unbending man. The other was Squire McGarrity. Squire McGarrity was the great man of New Kerry, that settlement of happy-go-lucky Irish, that district of ramshackle farms and fine horses and pretty girls. He was stocky and red-cheeked and white-haired, with the impish Irish humor glinting in his little blue eyes, and he was the law in New Kerry. There were many tales of his rule. One was about a fellow who got a lawyer all the way from Milltown to plead his case in the Squire's court, which was the McGarrity parlour. Nobody had ever done such a thing, and the Squire was not pleased. The Squire made a point, and the lawyer objected. "That's not the law," said the lawyer.

"Young feller," said Squire McGarrity, "I am the magistrate in New Kerry, and I make the law to suit the case. Sit down. Your client is fined five dollars, and his lawyer is warned agin contempt av this court. God save the Queen."

So father and I took Joe Tom and Molly to Squire McGarrity, with the Maltee boys rattling along behind in their old buggy for witnesses. My mother looked after the baby. It didn't take very long. As soon as the Squire knew what happened, he looked in my father's eyes, and you saw something passing there, the talk of good men that needs no words.

The Maltee boys deposed that Jim Ingleson had borrowed their gun to go hunting, that he had been drinking some stuff he made in a keg, and that was all they knew.

"Not by a jug-full," snorted the Squire, "but let it go. Joe Tom, what's your story?"

Joe Tom's eyes never left my father's face.

Father said quietly. "Go on, Joe Tom. Tell the Squire everything."

I'll omit the slow hobbling testimony of Joe Tom, his quaint accent, his outbursts in Micmac whenever his English failed, his mixed-up tale of events that Father and the Squire had to unscramble with kindly questions.

Briefly, it was what you know. Poor Molly was crazy about Ingleson, and thinking to please him she'd told about Joe Tom's source of wealth. Afterwards people declared that Ingleson had seduced her with that end in mind; but the man was incapable of looking so far ahead. Jim Ingleson was too worthless even to make a good villain.

What she couldn't tell him was the location. All Molly's wiles had failed to get that from Joe Tom. So at last, with a belly-full of Dutch courage and the borrowed gun—borrowed for what purpose no one but the dead man ever knew—Ingleson went to Joe Tom's, declared the child his, and Molly's heart as well. He had come to claim both, he said. The law would back him up, he said. No Injun had the right to a half-white girl, and him old, and she seventeen at the time; the marriage was illegal. He was glib, was Ingleson, and the words he used sounded like law in the Indian's ears. Then the loafer offered a bargain that shocked Joe Tom and Molly alike. Show him where the gold was. Show him that, and he would give up all claim to Molly and the child. He would give Joe Tom a paper to that effect. A paper. The Indians had a great respect for paper.

Did Ingleson threaten him with the gun, the Squire wanted to know.

Joe Tom answered honestly, no. He couldn't say what happened. He said his head seemed to swell. He heard himself shouting "*Kesnukwon!*" Now the word for liar in Micmac is *booskeeksooa;* but when you want to call a man a particularly-vile-scoundrel-of-a-liar you say *"Kesnukwon."*

At once they were struggling for the gun. Then Ingleson was lying on the floor, and Molly screaming that Joe had killed her Jeem, a white man, and would suffer for it. That was all he could remember.

The Squire called on the girl to testify, but sullenly she refused, as if she knew the law.

"Well," said Squire McGarrity, with his jaw up and his brogue coming thick, "it's a very simple case, after all. Here's a man, here's a spalpeen that gets himself dhrunk and goes out with a gun in the worst lightnin' storm we've had these ten years. There's trees struck right and left. There's Paddy Carrington's barn burt to the sod. There's the church hit, for all there's a lightin'-rod on the steeple. There's Regan's struck, and quare damage, with a pot knocked to pieces on the stove and divil a thing else. For lightnin' is quare stuff, that can whip a man's boots off, and him with no more than pins-and-needles down the leg—and on the other hand killed John O'Dwyer in his bed, three years back, without a scorch on his nightshirt, and ould Tress beside him complainin' cuz his feet's so cold. The Lord giveth and the Lord taketh away, and I don't see what's wrong with sain' a man died by act o' God. But some would object. So I'll put it that Jim Ingleson met his death by misadventure near Fairy Lake, Pine Country, at two by his first clock and wan-forty by the hindmost, in the afternoon av the sixth av July, in this year eighteen-hundhred-and-eighty-wan, and may God have mercy on his soul. Case dismissed."

Whatever folk thought of the Squire's court, the district was well rid of a scamp, it was agreed. A few grumbled, and thereafter pointed out Joe Tom as a murderer unhanged; but these were submerged for a time by the gold rush.

It began at New Kerry, where Joe Leahy found a nugget in a post-hole and uncovered what came to be known as the Leahy Vein. It was uncanny the way the news flew, in those days before rural telephones, in those days when railroads were still a-building, and you traveled by coasting schooner and then inland by coach over the rugged country roads. Men and boys deserted the farms, leaving crops to the women, or to rot in the ground; and it was no time before promoters were on the spot, and syndicates formed, and shares sold near and far, and machinery and experienced hardrock miners coming in from the States, and amateurs from all over the Maritimes and Newfoundland. Duncan's was the centre of attraction, for the Leahy Vein lay to southwest of it, and Shea's Prospect Vein to the north, and southeast along the post road three mines worked the Bar Hole Lode. Soon that quiet village of Scots farmers had a population of strangers in knee boots and red shirts, with three hotels, a Miners' Hall, a big livery stable, seven bars and a brothel. The quiet dark-eyed Syrians came, and Hebrews, and started shops where you could buy anything from a revolver to a beaver hat, and the manager of the Leahy Mine built himself out of company funds a mansion that cost fifteen thousand dollars, a prodigious sum. I could tell you tales that sound like Bret Harte, and you would smile. But they're true. It happened. A breath of Poker Flat in the Nova Scotia woods.

It lived ten years from first to last, but the boom was over in five. The old mining story—more money put into the ground than ever came out of it. The cost of mining those erratic and slender veins was terrific. They burnt a fortune in firewood alone, heating the boilers that ran the mine machinery, with an army of wood-cutters, Newfoundlanders, stripping the ridges for miles. Sometimes they struck another pocket like the one Leahy found, and hope flared up for a time. Then the cold truth sank in once more. And the deeper and colder the truth, the more men talked of Joe Tom and his mine. They believed he knew the mother lode, that Joe Tom's people had known it for centuries, and invented tales of a haunted lake to bar the road to it. The shores of Fairy Lake was scoured, and the old Indian graves desecrated, and you can still find, bush-choked, the pits and trenches they dug all over the wilderness.

The more unscrupulous began to pester Joe Tom, threatening "justice" for his "crime," and wheedling him with offers of partnership and protection. For a long time he had been watched whenever he stepped into the bush, and the Maltee boys, for their own ends, were amongst the spies. He dared not go near his "mine," wherever it was; but his grim Micmac humor led them many a merry dance in the wild country south and west of Fairy Lake. Eventually Molly grew tired of Joe Tom's poverty and ran off with a young Indian from Beaver River, who had come to work in the mines. No one in the lake country ever saw her or Jim Ingleson's child again. Old Joe Tom sat in his shack and brooded, and came now and again to my mother for something to eat; and my father went on with his farming, a sane man in Bedlam.

While this was going on I finished my studies and got a church in Cape Breton, and married a wife, and I didn't see Joe Tom again till the summer of '87. There was a guest at my father's; Donohue, the mining expert, brought in to write a post-mortem for the shareholders of the Leahy, and he went with me to Joe Tom's for the sake of the walk. Joe Tom had gone gray and shrivelled, as the Micmac men do when age strikes them at last, and walked with such a stoop that his big knotty hands hung to his knees. We talked for a bit. I didn't mention Molly, nor did he. He talked very little of anything; his English, always halting, seemed to have gone from him in his extreme age.

Just as we turned to go, he caught my arm and asked how long I planned to stay, calling me "Demsher" as he had always called my father.

"I leave in the morning," I said. It was pleasant to speak the tongue that was part of my childhood.

"A long time there is a stone in my heart," the old man said, "beacause of a thing hidden between thee and me. It makes a coldness, and it may that if I show this thing-which-is-hidden my heart will be warm again. For I have done evil, and have an evil reward in all things, and am the prey of evil men."

I thought he intended some revelation about the Ingleson affair, and tried to change the subject quickly, but he demanded "Come! We go!"

Joe Tom led the way across his pitiful fields (all choked with sorrel and quitch-grass, and all the fences down) and into the woods. We travelled a long time, much of it through black-spruce swamps, partly dried in the summer heat and buzzing with mosquitoes under the melancholy mop-headed trees. I lost all sense of direction, but I knew we must be moving in some roundabout fashion, for it was impossible to go so far in a straight line without striking one of the rounded glacial drifts where the farms were. We emerged into sunlight, and looked across a strip of wild meadow and a small sluggish brook to a slope studded with old stumps. It was faintly familiar, and suddenly I knew it for the north pasture of our own farm. I had seen this brook and scrap of wild meadow in the hollow as a boy, but from the other side of the pasture fence. Why had Joe Tom led me here in this furtive and uncomfortable way?

On the edge of the swamp, where the land began to rise towards the pasture, the ground was a tangle of fallen trees. Some of these windfalls were very old, the trunks and branches gone to moss-covered dust; others were as new as last September's gales. It was one of those places where trees grow to a good size and then blow down for lack of solid anchorage, and in falling turn up a great disc of roots and earth and clutched stones, like a dirty wicker basket-lid on edge, ten, fifteen or twenty feet high. After a year or two, ferns sprout all over the uprooted mass, and grass and small bushes, and the new circular wound in the earth is hidden by the overhang of alders, which always seem to spring up about such a place for such a purpose.

Joe Tom plunged into one of these thickets, and we found ourselves in the green gloom of a root cave. Six men could have stood upright in it. A spring seeped out of the foot of the hill and trickled amongst the exposed stones of the floor, and there was a sort of bowl which once had been full of gravel, for we could see its former contents scattered along the back of the cave amongst the roots.

"Demsher," Joe Tom said, "this is thine. Gold was here, and I took it. See! It was in the little stones, in the sand."

"What's he say?" Donohue asked with impatience.

I said, "He found gold in this place."

"Umph!" The mining man dropped to hands and knees and went all round, like a questing dog. There was a rusty shovel in a corner, and a rustier iron frying pan. Joe Tom's mining tools, unused for years. Donohue scooped some of the gravel into the pan and shook it industriously. After several pans, and still squatting, he looked up at me.

"Gold? Yes. He's pretty well cleaned it out, but there was a small pocket of nuggets and dust apparently. It came from that glacial drift where the farm sits, washed out by a stream under the ice-mass, back when the world was young. It means nothing. All these drumlins and kames contain a certain amount of gold, scraped off the outcrop in the ice age. If you dug the whole hill apart you might find another pocket or two; a thousand—maybe five thousand dollars' worth. But it'd cost you ten or twenty thousand before you were through. That's the curse of this whole district. Forget it. Let's get out of here before the mosquitoes eat us alive."

Donohue led the way up to the pasture, but Joe Tom held me back for a moment, and his old eyes were anxious. "Demsher, what says this man? Truly there is gold, much gold, the whole hill is gold? A little I have taken in my days of evil, but now that I have shown thee thy good fortune surely the evil goes from me?"

"Truly the hill is gold, Joe Tom. Thou hast but scratched it. Whatever thee took, that I give gladly from this my good fortune."

"And they will come now, the mining men?"

I shook my head. "More evil than good is in this gold. Like stinking meat, it is best covered with earth. If I give over my father's land to these men-moles, what then becomes of the crops, and the fruits, and the open door for the hungry? Guard thou thy tongue, as I guard mine. In time to come, when no harm can befall thee or me, or thy people and my people, then I shall tell of this gold."

That time has come.

Three Wise Men

Once upon a time there was a Division Superintendent with Notions. Don't shrug, brother, I'm aware that all Division Superintendents have them. But this one had notions of Economy—spelt with a big E. You see? There's a difference.

And every time the supply requisitions came in from his isolated stations in the Eastern Division, he sharpened his little blue pencil and covered those pathetic sheets with his little blue marks, cutting here, deleting there.

He knew—or thought he knew, which is just as good—how much canned meat would last four men a month, and how many desserts you could get out of a can of pineapple, and how many loaves were in a barrel of flour, and exactly the quantity of coal required to heat a windswept radio shack in the teeth of the wintry Atlantic.

And so it was that when the little supply steamer was held up by rough weather for days and weeks, as she often was and is, there were empty bellies and drawn belts in several bleak little radio shacks along the coast. There was the memorable time that Cape Ray ran short of provisions and waited days and days for the supply boat, which was unbeknown to them, hard and fast on the Labrador coast.

At intervals every day you'd hear them calling the steamer with never a sound of reply, because the old *Montmorency's* wireless man was huddled with the rest of the crew round a fire on the beach at Cocoacho Bay watching her break up. Then, after days of anxious waiting, came a message via Cape Race from the Division Superintendent, which ran:

'O. in C. Cape Ray. Reference your supply requisition. Consider quantity insect powder ordered excessive. Please advise.'

... a message which hangs to this day in a dinky little frame on the wall at Cape Ray for all to see and admire.

And the 'O. in C.'—Red Rory McBain himself—sent a reply which was picked up by a hundred aerials and convulsed the whole coast from Belle Isle to Cape Sable. And there were other stories.

But the story which will live the longest, because it is told with relish in wireless cabins on the Seven Seas and wherever radio men gather together, is the tale of Paddy Kerrigan, of Sable Island, and the Three Wise Men—one of whom was that same Division Superintendent; and it all happened back in the Dark Ages when the crystal detector was the Eighth Wonder of the World and men still spoke of Marconi's old 'magnetic' with tones of respect.

Paddy's fellow-exiles at the time were 'Matty' Wheeler—the same Matthew Wheeler who perished at his key in the wreck of the *Sarnia* years later; James 'Billums' Williams, who is now a Division Superintendent himself, blue pencil and all; and one 'erbert 'Nobby' Clark, the cockney cook. Four men living out the long days on a sand dune, a hundred miles off the Nova Scotia coast.

You know Sable Island, brother? A long sand-bar in the Atlantic; blasted by a pitiless sun in summer, swept with icy gales from Greenland in winter, and pounded all year round by a ceaseless surf that threatens its very existence. Littered with the wreckage of half a thousand ships and white with nameless bones; a grim spot, brother, without a tree to shade the sun or break the wintry wind. Just sand.

A desolate place, a God-forsaken place—the Graveyard of the Atlantic.

The steamer was due to leave Halifax with supplies, and there was revelry in the little shack, for Billums was going ashore. "Goin' ashore! Goin' ashore, me buckos," he shouted joyfully, snapping his fingers like castanets. "Ashore, me old stick-in-the-muds. Ashore, you bloomin' Robinson Crusoes. Tra-la-la, la-la, la-la." And he stepped gaily about the floor of the instrument room under the grim eyes of Kerrigan and Matty.

Mister 'erbert Clark appeared, polishing a plate with his apron. "Pipe down, ye ruddy canary," he said bitterly, " 'ave a 'eart."

Billums shook his head vigorously. "Not on your life, Nobby, me 'andsome darlin'," spinning dizzily on one toe like a rather clumsy ballet girl. "I've been here a blinkin year, my bold bucko, an' now I'm goin' ashore to make up for lost time. I'm goin' to live me some wild livin', Nobby, old thing."

He delivered an intricate caper around Matty and Kerrigan, eluding their clutching hands and leaped upon the operator's table, throwing himself into an attitude of oration.

"Friends and 'earers," he commented loftily, one hand thrust inside his shirt and one foot on the receiver tuning gear, "I who am about to leave salute thee." He blew them a kiss with his free hand. "Fast comes the shallop, beloved, which will bear me from your sight."

"Thank Gawd," breathed Matty.

"So 'appy am I," continued Billums, "that me 'eart is filled with music, and I feel I must burst forth in song."

"Burst somewhere else," suggested Paddy.

"So I shall entertain you," said the oblivious Billums, "With that very pathoose little song, 'I'll 'ang my 'arp on a weepin' willow tree'".

"Hang it on a sour apple tree an' be done with it," said Matty. Billums looked pained. "You do not, perhaps, approve my choice?" he asked. "Have you a suggestion? Another song, perhaps?"

"Sing, 'In the Blue Ridge Mountains of Virginia,' " said Kerrigan, jerking his thumb suggestively westward. "Or that good old 'ymn, 'I'm but a strynger 'ere, heaven is my 'hom,' " contributed Nobby.

Billums was very pained. "You are facetious idiots," he said, "But have no fear, beloved. *Vox populi, vox pei.* If you wish me not to sing, I shall not sing. I shall recite a little poem of my own, instead."

There were cries of "no, no," and "Spare us that", and a Hawk-head and Dowsett's Guide to Wireless Operators whacked with great violence against the wall behind him.

"A little poem, beloved, entitled, 'A Wireless Man's farewell to Sable Island.' Harrumff!"

They seized him with rude hands and bore him to the door and sat upon him heavily.

"The charges against the accused," intoned Kerrigan, sitting on Billum's chest, "are first: Singin' and Caperin' in such a manner as to disturb the public peace."

"Lemme gerrup," gurgled Billums.

"Second; endeavoring to spoud rotten poetry in the public ear."

"Currout, currout. Lemme up."

"Sergeant-at-Arms," said Kerrigan severely, "the court is noisy."

"Silence in the court," thundered Matty, seated on Billum's legs, and brought his palm down heavily on a projecting portion of the prisoner's anatomy.

"Third, an' most vile an' outrageous of all, gloatin'. Gloatin' in such a manner as to harrow the hearts of his feller men an' trample their tender feelin's in the dust."

"Sand," corrected the Sergeant-at-Arms.

"In the sand," amended the judge.

Lemme gerrup," choked the prisoner, near to strangulation.

"Gen'lemen," said His Honor seriously, "you all heard the charges agin the prisoner. You all witnessed his vile conduck. Jury, what is the verdick?"

Mister 'erbert Clark looked puzzled. "Wodge mean?"

"The jury," said His honor severely, "will quit wipin' dishes on its apron and bring in a verdict. And call me Your Honor, you blighter."

"Humph," said the jury importantly, "Guilty. Guilty, yer Honor."

"Good. Prisoner at the bar," pulling Billums' nose, "The verdict is guilty. I therefore condemn you to F.P. No. 4, according to the Sable Island Code. And may the Lord have mercy on your soul."

Wherefore they painted his nose with red ink and beat him unmercifully with a length of flexible insulator tubing.

It was Mister Nobby Clark who called them back to business. "These 'ere things," he said, fingering the head-phones dubiously, "seems to be awful noisy, 'ummin like a ruddy bumble bee."

And to their listening ears across the room came the faint drone of a non-synchronous spark calling "VCT, VCT, VCT."

"That'll be Halifax calling us," said Kerrigan, "Put the blinkers on, Matty."

Wheeler donned the phones, and they gathered about to watch his flying pencil.

Kerrigan, Officer, in Charge, Sable Island.

Steamer sails to-days. Party officials, eastern division, aboard. Will inspect your station. Party includes Mr. Gale, engineer, Mr. Gabriel Tuppit, secretary, II. Bedford Rowe, Division Superintendent.

There was a perturbed silence in the little room.

"Mister Roarin' Gale, Mister Angel Gabriel Tuppit, and Mister Emperor William Rowe hisself," jeered Kerrigan, waving the blue form. "Three Wise Men out of the East!" And he minced around the room examining the switchboard, the rotary spark and the top of Wheeler's head with an imaginary magnifying glass.

"Bloomin' bureaucrats," said Billums, "Can't you see 'em steppin' around the dunes and sniffin' the invigoratin' salt air and tellin' us what a glorious life we have here? Can't you, just?"

"Some of them 'ead blokes, eh?" said Nobby, "ruddy red tabs," for Nobby had served his time in the British army.

Billums said vindictively: "Hope they get their feet wet gettin' ashore. Hope they get upset in the surf, the pryin' stiffnecks."

Paddy Kerrigan wagged an admonitory forefinger. " 'ats *lese majeste*, me bucko." He pronounced it Lazy Majesty. "Naughty, naughty!" He wished the same himself.

When the steamer *Lady Laurier* arrived off the island, it looked almost as if the Wise Men might indeed get their feet wet, for the surf was growling on the bars and the sea was steadily getting up. Old Captain Havers took one look at the gleaming line of surf and shook his head. "Can't land an ounce of stores in that," he said grimly.

"Why not?" snorted Mister Roarin' Gale.

The skipper's eye travelled coolly up and down the length of Mr. Gale. "Because you can't. Can't land stores on that island with any degree of safety unless the sea's dead calm. And right now it ain't."

"Why not?" snorted Mister Roarin' Gale.

"I see," said Mr. Gale, meaning that he didn't.

"See that light streak on the water, Mister Gale? 'Tween us and the shore. That's a submerged bar. In calm weather you can ease a loaded boat over it all right; you may scrape a little but it don't matter. But when the surf is up, mister, the waves shoot across that bar like express trains and carry a boat along with 'em. Now a few men in a boat don't matter; they'll get a fast ride ashore on the crest of the surf and shoot 'way up the beach like one of them board-riders at Waikiki.

But a loaded boat, mister, that's different. A loaded boat is apt to ketch her bow on the bar and flap right over with the force of them waves under her stern. I've seen some mighty bad spills right there, Mister Gale."

"Hmmm," said Gale, obviously unimpressed. "You say a few men in a boat are safe enough. Couldn't you land Tuppit and Rowe and myself right now? We'd get our inspection over as soon as possible and be back aboard in a jiffy. Our time's valuable, captain."

The skipper rubbed his chin and looked again at the distant line of white water. "I can set you ashore, all right," he said slowly, "but you'll have to make that inspection snappy, mister. No use me hangin' around here if I can't land my stuff, and I don't like the look of the weather, myself."

A little group at the base of the radio mast watched the boat pass the bar. "How come?" puzzled Wheeler; "surf gettin' up and a mean look in the sky and here's these birds comin' ashore."

"S'pose my relief man's there?" chattered the eager Billiums, "s'pose I ought to pack my ditty box?"

"Pipe down," said Nobby-the-cook. "Four men at the oars. Big 'un in the stern'll be the *Laurier's* bosun. Three men stannin' aft'll be the Three Blokes. No, m'son, yer relief is still aboard, waitin' a dry-foot chance ashore s'likely."

Billums' face fell.

"I'd say Mister Roarin' Gale had bullied Havers into settin' 'em on the beach," suggested Kerrighan. "They'll figure to rush this inspection job and get back aboard before the surf gets too bad. Then old Havers beats it back to the mainland to wait for better weather, they'll step ashore. Neat, I calls it."

The boat ran up the beach easily and three figures stepped out over the bow, padded around in the sand awhile, and then headed towards the wireless station.

Kerrigan was whistling softly a lilting Irish tune. The significance of this was lost upon the other watchers until Matty realized suddenly that the tune was 'Banks o' Boyne'. 'Banks o' Boyne' was not a song to Kerrigan, it was a state of mind.

"War song," shouted Matty triumphantly; "Paddy's war song."

He seized Kerrigan by the coat lapels and shook him. "Out with it, you Irish schemer; what's to do?"

Kerrigan's eyes were fixed on space, "Risin' swell from the no'theast," he said softly, "and makin' up to blow like fury. Glass droppin' like lead. Old Havers hoppin' up and down his bridge like a Kilkenny cat on hot bricks. Supposin', just supposin', those Three Wise Omadhauns get most might interested in little hauns get most mighty interested in little old VCT and forget the time. Old Havers won't wait one blinkin' unnecessary minute with a no'theaster brewin' and the Graveyard on his lee. Not for the whole Department of Marine an' Fisheries, let alone three measly Marconi wallahs."

"Well, s'posin'," said Matty impatiently. "What then?"

"Then," said Kerrigan sweetly, "then the Three Wise Men will be guests at our 'umble 'ome until the weather improves. Which may be two, three, perhaps four or even five days, if the gods be kind."

Nobby-the-cook was troubled. "Yus," he said, dubiously, "but look 'ere Paddy, what we goin' to feed 'em with? All we got is salt 'orse and murphies.

Kerrigan swept off his cap and bowed low. "'Tis a wise men ye are, Nobby me bucko. Ye have it. All we got is salt 'orse and murphies."

With glad outcry they thumped him on the back and shook his hands and pulled his cap down over his eyes hard, so that he just pried it off in time to see the three perspiring inspectors topping a nearby dune and approaching.

There were mutual introductions and handshakes; condescension on one side and humble servility on the other.

"Tell me," said the tall, bespectacled Angel Gabriel Tuppit, unpleasantly, "how is it that your entire—ah—staff's—ah—off duty?"

Wheeler scuttled into the shack like a frightened rabbit. They heard the pop-pop of the gasoline exhaust and the air was rent with the ear-splitting rotary spark.

"A momentary laxity of discipline," explained Kerrigan, feeling very red and hot about the ears. "We felt we all ought to be out to welcome you, gentlemen."

"Quite so, Kerrigan, quite so. Ha!" rasped H. Bedford Rowe. "An entirely excusable sentiment—ha!—but don't let it happen again, eh Mr. Tuppit?"

They passed into the little building and were soon immersed in the apparatus. Mr. Roarin' Gale took the lead and poked his pugnacious nose into everything. He was an engineer—a radio engineer, what's more—and wanted 'em to know it, by gad!

With meticulous care he examined the big marine gas-engine that drove the dynamo. He ran this thick finger along the belts and said they used too much dope; he didn't like the way they spliced them either. Did they ever clean the cummutator and cut down the micas? And how about the slip-rings? And the emergency battery? Ever change the high tension oil in the transformer? Or condensers? What was their radiation? Power input? Gas consumption? Wasn't that excessive?

And so on, H. Bedford Rowe supplementing—ha!—now and again and poor old Kerrigan explaining and apologizing, and listening in agony for the first impatient toot of the *Lady Laurier's* whistle.

He never heard it, or the next half-dozen either. There was a lot of noise there in the little shack, what with the pop-popping of the engine and the slapping of the belts and the whirr of the generator, and the terrific crash-crash of the open spark as Matty feverishly plied the big brass key.

The wind was moaning in the aerials and whirling the sand outside pretty briskly when they finally heard a long blat from seaward, and Mr. Tuppit said quickly: "That is the steamer. They wish us to return." Kerrigan's heart sank. Their little dream was to be shattered, then. The shack at Sable Island is set in the hollow of some big dunes, so he could not know that old Havers had recalled his boat-crew and pulled up his hook; that the long blat was a gesture of farewell and that the *Lady Laurier* was chugging for White Head as fast as she could chug.

Kerrigan helped the Wise Men to gather up their brief cases and other impedimenta and left the shack with them; Mr. Roarin' Gale keeping up a running fire of criticism on the way, and Angel Gabriel Tuppit running ahead and urging them to hurry. But their haste was needless, for when they topped the dune the sea was empty and old Havers' smoke a mere blob on the horizon. Little Billums fled into the shack with the news, and developed an alarming hysteria so that Wheeler had to lay aside the phones and stuff his mouth with the best part of the Proces-Verbal pad to keep him quiet.

For two days and nights a northeaster lashed the sea to fury and whirled great clouds of sand along the island that blinded and brought blood to the cheek. And for two days the three inspectors ate salt-'orse and murphies, breakfast, dinner and supper.

They put a good face on it at first, old Emperor William saying hilariously that "a little diet of plain honest food—ha!—would be the finest thing in the world for them."

But after the third meal the joy went right out of it and they began losing appetite and Mr. Roarin' Gale commenced making semi-audible remarks about the unmentionable circumstances which had landed him on this unmentionable place. One gathered that Captain Havers of the *Lady Laurier* was a 'sippy-sappy old woman,' of whose parentage on the male side Mr. Gale was extremely doubtful.

Kerrigan was greatly distressed, of course. The fare was, he admitted, terrible; but the fact was they'd run out of grub about a week or so ago. Funny thing about that; they'd economized on their grub just as Mister Rowe had told them. Here Messrs. Gale and Tuppit cocked eyebrows at H. Bedford Rowe so that he squirmed uneasily and bolted a whole mouthful of salt-horse.

But there it was, they'd run out just the same. Take last year, now, they'd had roast duck and mighty nice, too—and the Three Wise Men looked up hopefully—but the ducks wouldn't arrive on the island for several weeks yet. They migrated from the north at the first cold weather and wintered on the island. Too bad! Roast duck would taste mighty good right now; still, salt beef wasn't so bad when you got used to it. The first week was the hardest.

And so on.

On the third morning the wind went down and the Wise Men wore a track over the dunes from the station to the beach to see if the surf was going down. It stayed perversely and distinctly up, roaring and pounding along the twenty-six mile length of the island, and toward evening they gave up their disconsolate patrol, for they found that the sand got into their shoes and chafed their feet raw.

Kerrigan and Matty armed themselves with staves from a heavy cask and sneaked up on a big seal that was sunning itself high up the beach, and killed it with neat blows—ponk—ponk—one on each side of the skull, just like that. And Nobby served it up that night, for a 'chynge', as he said.

You know seal meat, brother. You soak it and steam it and lavish all your culinary arts upon it and when you're all done it tastes just like a greasy bunch of seaweed.

Hope died away from the Three Wise Men as they chewed upon their first mouthful. Gale thrust his plate away from his with undisguised disgust, and it was Angel Gabriel Tuppit who suggested that, 'as the choice of two evils, as it were—ah!' he 'preferred the salt beef.'

"It ain't werry appetisin'," admitted Nobby from the kitchen doorway. "Nah them Newfunlanners claims as 'ow they kin myke it tyste like chickin. But I dunno, I dunno. Any people wot kin live orf of dry cod arf the year is larble to think this is patty-de-foy-grass." And he shook his head mournfully.

Kerrigan felt real bad about the seal meat. Now the boat before last had been delayed, he said, and they'd rubbed along very nicely on seal meat and gull eggs. Great stuff, gull eggs. You invaded a gull colony with a gunny sack and gathered the eggs while another fellow kept the gulls off with a long pole. Not a pleasant job; for the gulls had a habit of poising over your head and then dropping like a plummet, beak fist, on top of it. And you had to test the eggs in a bucket of water and the ones that sank were the 'fresh' ones—and even those tasted a bit addled, Mister Gale. "But, of course, you don't mind that when you're hungry," smiling sweetly at H. Bedford Rowe.

That night the wind sprang up from the northwest and raked the landing beach from the opposite corner, as it has a fashion of doing at

Sable Island. Matty, on the midnight watch, heard it howling through the mast stays and grinned to himself.

Four days, five days. Kerrigan confessed to Billums that if the ruddy boat'd only turn up and land some real grub he'd gladly forego the pleasing spectacle of the discomfited wise men. At noon meal on the fifth day, Billums broke a grim silence around the table. "My blinkin' wisdom tooth is bleedin'," he said. The others grunted and the silence fell again.

Billums dabbed at his tooth with a none-too-clean handkerchief—you are your own laundryman at Sable Island—and examined the faint bloodstains with detached interest. As he went to thrust the grubby rag back into his trousers he happened to glance up and meet the strangely intense glance of Kerrigan. He was startled.

"Scurvy!" shouted Paddy, triumphantly.

"Scurvy!" echoed Nobby, staring aghast at the unfortunate Billums.

"Scurvy!" ejaculated the horried Wise Men.

"Scurvy, Scurvy," muttered Billums; "what the—?"

He had received a violent kick on his shin under the table.

"Open your mouth," commanded Kerrigan.

Billums opened his capacious mouth, displaying an excellent set of teeth.

"Bleedin' all over his gums," announced Kerrigan, with a prodigious wink at Bilums. "D'ye feel tired?"

Billums, inwardly illuminated by a sudden great light, admitted a tired feeling.

"Regular exhaustion," suggested Kerrigan, "slowly comin' on?"

"I've noticed regular exhaustion," admitted Billums slowly, and added that it had been creeping on for some time.

"I've noticed it, too," declared Kerrigan, with the face of a graven image.

They put the protesting Billums to bed, where he promptly developed a violent delirium, reciting his Farewell Poem over and over again monotonously and barking like a dog and yowling cat-fashion and asking the mystified Mr. Tuppit why he didn't blow his horn.

Kerrigan sat at the head of the bed, smoothing the sick one's pillow and generally soothing him. The Three Wise Men stood at the foot of the bed watching gloomily, and starting back nervously at every Dervish howl from the stricken Billums.

The delirium became steadily worse, in spite of all that Kerrigan could do.

"Meat," said Billums, licking his lips with a large pink tongue and rolling his eyes crazily; "nice, juicy, red meat. Lovely meat. Beautiful meat. Nice fresh tender meat, all drippin' an' bloddy." And he gnashed his strong teeth.

The Wise Men edged nearer to the door.

Billums counted them with outstretched forefinger. "One, two, three, four," he said; and again; "One, two, three, four."

Then he began counting on his fingers, "One, two, three, four," glaring at his hand with his eyes hideously crossed.

"Salt Beef an' 'taters! Salt Beef an' 'taters! Ha-ha-ha-ha. Ha-ha-ha-ha-ha!" and the shack rang with maniacal laughter.

He turned to Kerrigan. "You are my mother," he said, staring fixedly at Paddy's face. "No. No, you're not, either. Your face is too ugly. You are my Aunt Sarah," and before Kerrigan could dodge, Billums seized him and twined a sinewy arm about his neck and kissed him noisily three times. The Wise Men fled, shaking their heads.

"Salt beef an' 'taters. Salt beef an' 'taters," yelled Billums after them. "Ha-ha-ha-ha-ha!"

Kerrigan's solicitous air vanished. He cuffed Billums soundly, jammed a pillow over his face and delivered a breath-taking jab into his 'midships section. "Pipe down!" he hissed, "Pipe down, ye blitherin' ass."

"Ugh!" said Billums, indignant, "S'mar rer?"

"You're layin' it on too thick, that's what."

Billums was annoyed. "Say, you," he said. "Who's having' this scurvy anyway, huh? You or me?"

"You are," said Paddy, "you've havin' it an' I'm directin' it. I'll have you know this was my own bright idea, me bucko. And very nicely it's worked out so far. But not so thick, Billums boy, not so thick. Old Angel Gabriel looks a trifle suspicious to me."

"Right," grunted Billums in a satisfied tone.

"But I can whoop a little now an again, eh?" he asked anxiously.

Kerrigan nodded. There was a sound of footsteps outside the room. H. Bedford Rowe had been sent to reconnoitre.

"Meaow. Meaooooow. Meaoooooow," yowled Billums, "Salt beef an' 'taters. Ha-ha-ha-ha-ha-ha-ha-ha."

They held a council of war that night in the instrument room, after the delirious Billums had sunk into slumber, and it was agreed all round that they would all die like poisoned rats if the steamer didn't soon arrive.

"We might shoot a wild pony," suggested Kerrigan hopefully. "Lots of wild pones down the island. 'Member, Wheeler, last winter when the boat got hung up?"

"Do I?" declared Matty unblushingly, "Say, that was the time we had boiled horse-meat for our Christmas dinner."

The Wise Men shuddered. Mr. Roarin' Gale announced flatly that he preferred scurvy to horsemeat, and that speaking for himself he'd stick to the salt meat and potatoes.

And stick they did, all of them.

Gale, as superior, decreed that H. Bedford Rowe should take Billums' place at the key—Rowe having declared in a rash moment that he could 'pound brass with the best on the coast.'

So they were treated to the spectacle of Rowe-Emperor Williams Rowe—wrestling with the big gas engine and getting his dandified person all grease and dirt; Rowe hopelessly roasted by the swift brass-pounders at Cape Race and North Sydney and Halifax and Cape Sable, and begging them to 'Q.R.S.'—send slower—the white flag of the ether; Rowe sending chronic morse with a hand that fairly trembled on the key, so that a cheeky operator on some outbound tramp begged him to 'Use the other foot.'

Six days, seven days. On the morning of the seventh, the sea began to subside and the glass rose fast, and Matty called the *Lady Laurier* with the news. And he offered an inward prayer of thankfulness as the *Laurier's* sputtering spark told him that she was on her way.

There was no sign of salt 'orse or murphies when they sat down to their last meal together.

"Gentlemen," said Kerrigan sorrowfully, "our supply of salt beef is, I regret to say, exhausted."

Relief flitted over the faces of the Three Wise Men. It was obvious that salt 'orse was a poor substitute for hunger, to them.

"However," proceeded Kerrigan, with the air of a chef announcing the piece de resistance, "Our cook has a new delight for us."

And Nobby, as a sort of parting culinary triumph, served up a roast gull. A huge, leathery mackerel-gull, whose aroma was vaguely reminiscent of split cod drying on the Nova Scotia fish-flakes in a hot sun. A big bird, a rare bird. A bird which had undoubtably lived a long, hard life.

Kerrigan went at it with reckless Irish courage; Angel Gabriel Tuppit and the Division Superintendent toyed with it gingerly. But the effect upon Mr. Roarin' Gale was simply astounding.

He leaped to is feet and hurled his offensive portion to the far corner of the room, plate and all; and he uttered a big round word in a big round voice. And he proceeded to tell the world in general and H. Bedford Rowe in particular just what he thought of V.C.T. and the island it stood on and the government steamers and the gross idiocy that had put H. Bedford Rowe in a position of responsibility.

One gathered that Mr. Rowe was a soulless ass, a nincompoop, a half-wit and a menace to the Eastern Division, and as for his little blue pencil—!

Rowe, it seemed, was among other things, a sanguinary lunatic, without a single unprintable atom in sense in his whole unprintable carcass; positively and persistently starving these poor unprintable men for the sake of his own still more unprintable credit at Head Office.

And very much more in the same strain.

"Blimy," muttered Nobby, awe-stricken, "Ain't 'eard the likes of 'im since I left the awmy."

"Now the joke av ut," said Kerrigan, telling the story to me afterward, "was this." Kerrigan was Dublin University and 'quality' but lapsed into the brogue at times as you see.

"The new Divvy Soop who replaced old Emperor William had that very same notion, begob. Economy with the big E. So the joke was on ourselves after all. And Rowe? Rowe disappeared until the War broke out a year or two aftherward, Jimmy McNeil, of the steamer

Mercy, it was who got word av the scut in Rotterdam. The *Mercy* ye'll mind was a Belgian Relief packet. Seems old Emperor William had a job with the Relief Commission on the Dutch frontier, handin' out rations to the shtarvin' Belgians. Upon me soul!"

The Pay-Off at Duncan's

Jordan and I came bowling into Duncan's Corner at twenty-five miles an hour, and the village curs scattered from our path to yap a greeting that hung in the frosty air like puffs of smoke. We had a feeling of triumph, as though this motor trip through thirty miles of snow-bound timberland were an epic of some sort. The truth was that the Company had kept the road open with snowploughs to permit movement of pulpwood in motor-trucks to their big mill at River Harbour, and our narrow passage through the timber was paved with hard packed snow that gave smoother riding than many a town street. Light steel chains fastened to the rear wheels over the tyres gave excellent traction on this arctic pavement, and a half-and-half mixture of alcohol and water in the radiator secured the cooling system of the little car against freezing.

The engine had purred all the way like a satisfied cat, to the accompaniment of a faint clink-clink of tyre chains and the peculiar hissing 'reeeep!' of rubber on snow. There had been incidents, of course. Four times we skidded out of the ploughed track and plunged into roadside drifts, where the driving wheels spun helplessly in the snow. Not the soft flaky sort that makes good snowballs, you understand, but harsh cold-weather snow like coarse salt that gripped the car and refused to pack. There had been much pushing and grunting, the chain-bound tyres hurling snow into my strained face, while Jordan sat at the wheel with his big larrigan-shod foot jammed on the accelerator. Once we had to tramp back some distance to summon the crew of a lumber camp to our aid, and these huskies had picked up the car—Jordan and all—and dumped it back in the road with a single shoot of "Up she goes!" For the rest, it was like swimming miraculously through a gigantic Christmas card, the stark hardwoods and snow-mantled pine and spruce rolling past in a mosaic of brilliant sunshine and indigo shadow. We were three hours on the road.

Duncan's is a group of twenty or thirty wooden buildings sprawling about a cross-roads in the "No'thern Deestrict" of Pine County. There is a Masonic Hall (where Joe M'Intyre shows moving pictures once a week), a church, a barber's shop and a garage with two bright red gasolene pumps. Bill Nolan's hotel stands at the cross-roads proper; a square wooden box with shady verandahs, a red roof and white-painted shingles—blinding in the winter sunlight—staring you in the face as you enter Duncan's from the south. Then there is a store labelled DOUGLAS BROS. on one of the strategic corners, dull red with bright blue door and window-frames. Upon the other is PARREL'S GROCERY, more modest in green and white, but marred by a huge daub over one wall advertising somebody's tobacco.

The surrounding district was settled after the War of 1812 by optimistic Scots from the disbanded British regiments, and the farms they hewed out of a howling wilderness are perched on the sterile flank of a ridge running from the Corner into the backwoods. Their hardships must have been terrific, for Pine County soil is stony, bitter stuff, fit for Nature's own crop of timber and little else. Their descendants still plough the windy hillsides, cutting saw-logs and pulpwood on their own timber lots in the winter-time, and shopping at the Corner on Saturday nights, though many have drifted away to the States and other scenes more prosperous. Ruined farmhouses gape at you, old stone-walled pastures growing up into thickets of spruce and fir, and you can hunt deer in abandoned orchards from Duncan's to the shores of Rossignol. *Odoccoileus Virginianus* is partial to sour apples.

At some time in the credulous 'nineties of the last century, Duncan's was the scene of a gold-mining rush, a petty flurry that arose, boomed and fizzled in three years of golden fireworks. The only mark it left on Duncan's (except a few heaps of tailings hidden in the bush and a mouldering pit or two) was George Barrish. George, full of youthful optimism, had trekked over the old wagon road to Duncan's with a small printing press in the back of his cart (seeing himself as the Voice of the People in the new Eldorado) and started a weekly newspaper called 'The Northern District Gold Hunter.' When the boom petered out he had added '& Farmer's Advocate' to the title and stayed on, selling fancy buggies and riding wagons to the farmers as a side line. George was a landmark.

We pulled up outside George's little wooden shop with a squeal of frosty brakes and a final 'Reeep!'' of snow under the tyres, waving mittened hands in greeting to a shadowy George seen dimly through the frost of the window-pane. In a trice the door was flung open, and George himself stood there in his shirt-sleeves, sublimely indifferent to the frigid air of the street. "Come in, boys," thundered the Gold Hunter and Farmer's Advocate. In we went, to stamp our larrigans on the worn plank floor and warm frost-bitten fingers over a red-hot stove. The home of 'The Northern District Gold Hunter & Farmer's Advocate' was a one-storey shack, a long shadowy room full of ancient printing apparatus. A bright-faced youngster was printing Christmas cards on the small job press, trimming the edges with a ponderous guillotine; and George's daughter, Jeanie, was setting up type for the next edition and getting her thin fingers infamously dirty in the process. With their exception you saw the Gold Hunter office precisely as it was in the halcyon days after old Micah Henneberry found a nugget in a post-hole and put Duncan's briefly but gloriously on the map. Everything in that warm little shack was a museum piece, even to the owner's pipe, which had an ancient and noisome smell.

George sucked a mouthful of smoke from this dudeen and blew it up among the rafters. "Well," he said, "so you've come to pay off the lumberjacks." We had. The men were coming out from the Rossignol pulpwood camps for Christmas, and we were to pay their little 'Wages Due' slips and speed them on their way. There were a number of Pine

County men, most of whom would be taking the southern road over which we had come; the rest would head for the railway at New Germany, twenty miles or so to the eastward. The farmer's advocate looked up at the smoke curling among the dusty rafters with enormous interest. "Didn't bring cash with you?" I shook my head and twisted my mouth in that sidewise grimace which means, Emphatically No. I said, "Too risky. They'd like to have cash, no doubt, but they'll have to take cheques. Shouldn't need any money till they reach town, anyway. Most of 'em have a little money in their pockets."

"You're durn right," said George soberly. He walked to the stove and spat against the red-hot iron. "Risky stuff, cash. Where you goin' to pay 'em, boys?" Jordan jerked a thumb. "Marsdon hired an empty shack down by the barber's. It's got a stove and a place where we can sit down and do a bit of writing."

"Uh-huh," grunted George. He blew out another poisonous stream. "Seen 'em yet?"

There was something in the way he said this. "No—why?" demanded Jordan and I together.

"Nothin'." George made a horizontal motion with his pipe, as if to sweep our sudden interest aside. "Nothin' much."

"Except——?" I prompted.

"Yeah," Jordan said. "Let's hear the bad news, George."

"Well, boys, there's nothin' very much. They came outa the camps yesterday, expectin' you fellers would be here, I guess. That's thirty miles over the tote-road. Some of 'em took a chance an' crossed Rossignol on the ice, but the ice ain't very safe this early in the season; most of 'em tramped all the way round by the tote-road. An' nobody here to pay 'em."

Jordan grinned confidently. "They had to come out some time, George."

"They won't mind," I said. "They're going home for Christmas."

"No-o-o," mused George. " 'Course, there ain't much accommodation here for two hundred men, boys. Most of 'em slept in barns last night." He paused for a significant moment. "Kinda frosty last night. For so early in the winter, I mean. Ten or twelve below."

"A mistake," I explained. "We sent word by Marsdon that we'd be here to-day, and here we are. But, after all, what do they care?"

"Yeah," drawled Jordan. "If they had to sleep on the soft side of a plank last night it's their own funeral."

"Sure," George agreed reasonably. "But you're goin' to have an interestin' pay-off, boys. Y'can betcha life on that. Y'see, some enterprisin' bootlegger blew in last night with a lotta bad booze. Feller from New Germany way, I guess."

We whistled, Jordan and I, without harmony. The shadow of coming events was cast before us.

Most of the lumberjacks were our own Pine County men, or pleasant hard-working 'Dutchmen' from the neighbouring Alsace County, but hard times had driven a strange new element into the camps. There were out-of-work miners from the Cape Breton coalfields, steel workers from the Sydney plants, apple farmers from the Valley earning a little cash in the unproductive winter months, city rats from mean Halifax streets, stranded sailors, clerks and mechanics down on their luck and a number of hoboes shipped (with one-way fare) to the lumber woods by harassed relief committees. English, French, Scots, Irish and German descent—a cross-section of the provincial population—with a sprinkling of bohunks, the nomad Poles, Russians and Czechs. Many of these had never swung an axe before. At so much per cord of wood, cut, sawn and piled, these greenhorns earned meagre wages at the expense of sore hands and aching muscles, and the camp deductions for board and small supplies like mittens and tobacco would leave them very little at the pay-off.

There had been lamentation over this, we knew. There had even been rumours of 'red' talk in the camps, for some of the malcontents had quit and tramped out to River Harbour for their wages, filling our quiet air with their discontent and their sour unwashed smells. It mattered little that experienced men were able to clear three dollars a day at the maligned piece-rate, for your true lumberjack is a born 'kicker', and it was only human that he should absorb some of this unrest. As for Jordan and myself, it was obvious that we, the present and visible signs of the distant and invisible Company, would be the chief objects of their wrath. Two hundred husky lumberjacks were waiting around the corner for their pay, each of whom had hiked long miles through the woods to Duncan's, spent the night in a chilly barn and acquired a bellyful of smuggled rum in the morning.

"Yep," repeated the proprietor of the 'Gold Hunter' with his air of complete detachment. "She's goin' to be an interestin' pay-off."

We buttoned up our mackinaws, thanked George for his tip and sallied forth to face the music.

Outside the hired shack, the village street was filled with men in mackinaws of gaudy, checkerboard pattern, green, black, brown, red and yellow, and breeches of mackinaw cloth or trousers of heavy black frieze. Some wore heavy homeknit stockings, pulled over their trouser-legs and gartered below the knee with string; the rest wore their breeches *on plein*, as a sort of arctic jhodpurs. 'Lumbermen's rubbers' were fairly general, though there were plenty of moccasins and high-laced larrigans, and each man had a huge pair of woollen mittens on his hands or tucked into his belt. There were one or two moth-eaten fur caps and a number of battered fedoras, but the general wear was a stocking cap of red or blue wool, pulled down over the ears. In this garb, much torn and rudely patched, they made a vivid picture against the background of snow, kaleidoscopic with their restless movement. Each carried his small belongings strapped upon his shoulders in a gunny-bag or pack of some sort, with here and there the worn khaki of an army knapsack, relic of the Strange Interlude. Without exception they were bearded. Four camps, and not a razor. Red beards, black beards, blond beards, pepper-and-salt beards, the growth of many weeks and months. Here and there an attempt had been made to trim this rampant hairiness. Tonsorially speaking, the Grand Duke Nicholas, the Third Napolean, Kaiser Wilhelm, Lord Dundreary, General Burnside and Admiral von Tirpitz were all present, in mackinaws and bull's wood trousers; but the common run were plain unbridled whiskers, looking, Jordan muttered, "like last year's bird-nests."

The men greeted our appearance with a ragged cheer in which there was an undercurrent—a sub-discord, so to speak—of whistles and catcalls, and opened their crowd to let us gain the door, closing in behind us again like a wall. The shack was a simple affair of hemlock boards, perhaps twenty feet square, with a tarred-paper roof, a rude plank floor, and a single window, broken by some impatient fist. Near the door stood a squat box stove, glowing red, with seven or eight feet of rusty chimney-pipe extending to the ceiling; otherwise the furniture consisted of a shelf beneath the window and a pair of rickety chairs. The place was filled to bulging-point with men. We thrust a way to the window-shelf with swimming motions and shouts of "Gangway, boys!" and found Marsdon there, the big, drawling, grey-haired boss of the camps, with his papers and accounts. I pulled cheques, blotters, ink and pen from my knapsack and took a seat.

"All right, boys," Jordan said. "Who's first?"

There was a single murmur in the crowded room and a single movement; men pressed forward until Marsdon and I, seated on the crazy chairs, were forced to brace our larrigan-shod feet against the wall to resist the pressure. A shower of 'Wages Due' slips fluttered down upon the shelf in a blizzard of grubby flakes. I stripped off my gloves and began to scrawl cheques with a warm blast of human breath, redolent of rum, sweeping over my shoulders. The pay-off went slowly. Each man had his slip, provided by the clerk of his camp, and signed by Marsdon showing his wages and the various deductions for board and supplies from the 'Van', and with this chit before me I wrote the cheque in payment and signed it with my galloping signature. Before this could be accomplished, however, the men insisted on checking over each item with Marsdon's copies of the various camp accounts, as was their right; for they had all the manual labourer's suspicion of ink and paper, and it mattered nothing that the camp clerks had gone through the same weary business. Marsdon, patience in the flesh, called out the items in his slow deep voice, and each man repeated them after him, like a child at catechism. Those who "had no learnin' " usually followed this by staring ox-like at the mystic black-and-white of Marsdon's accounts for several dumb seconds before turning to some scholar in the crowd with a brusque, "That right, Mac? Huh?"

It took time—an enormous amount of time. And the crowd itself, jostling and impatient, swearing and arguing in a rising chorus, did nothing to speed the business. The little stove, filled with split birch and maple, glowed brighter with the passing minutes, and the tin chimney-pipe turned from rust to a dull cherry colour for half its length. The atmosphere became terrific, for we worked in a blue fog of tobacco smoke, and the peculiar smell of the lumber camp—damp cloth, cheap tobacco, balsam and sweat—arose in the heat and confinement like a Fundy tide. Hot gusts of raw Demerara, the cheap smuggled rum known to the camps as 'tiger sweat,' eddied in the maelstrom. I wrenched off my warm mackinaw and thanked Joss for the broken window.

I knew, if we could pay this restless mob quickly, that we might avert any serious trouble. With cheques in their pockets and the magic of Christmas-at-home their mood must turn more cheerful, their grievances, real and imaginary, assume a just proportion. But there is very little sense of humour in tiger sweat, and no sense of proportion at all in men possessed of it, and the insufferable delay of the pay-off, though of their own making, proved a last and fatal straw. The little room was soon filled with angry voices howling "Give us our money!" The crowd began to surge to and fro, a swirling, impotent movement set up by men fighting their way toward Marsdon, Jordan and me, by the paid men trying to fit their way out, and by the roaring mob outside thrusting burly shoulders into the jammed doorway. The whole shack quivered; it seemed actually to bulge, a boiler filled with rising force, without a safety valve. But at this point a valve appeared. Not a safety valve, of course, but at least a valve.

A squat, quiet man dropped his due-bill at my elbow for payment. Jan Karosny, said the due-bill, fifty dollars and twenty-two cents. A Hungarian soldier who had drifted, as had many of his comrades, to Canada after the war, he had a great bayonet scar across his cheek (received at the hands of a raging moujik in some wild scrimmage in the Carpathians) and a corresponding lack of teeth in that side of his mouth, which compelled him to chew his tobacco on the other. Promptly a hoarse voice, redolent of rum, bellowed over my shoulder, "Hey! It's my turn"; and I turned in the rickety chair to behold an angry bearded face glaring at the stolid Jan, and a great bony fist waving in vague circles, between them. "My turn," said Jan. The shack was filled with sudden menace. The Hungarian shifted his feet a little, a barely perceptible movement, and a voice shouted, "Look out! He's got a knife." At this point Christensen, the big blond Swede, deserter from a tramp in Halifax harbour, tapped Jan on the shoulder. "Better you shod op," he suggested.

Jan was a Camp Four man; Christensen was from Camp Two. A fist shot out of the surging ring, and the blond sailor went down under the trampling feet. (Afterwards we carried him out and loaded him like a sack of meal upon a motor truck. There were little drops of bright blood, like beads, in his golden beard.) At once there was a convulsion.

Fists flew. All over the crowded floor stamped a hundred feet; the dull thump of lumbermen's rubbers, the clop-clop of frost-hardened shoe-packs, the hissing shuffle of oil-tanned moccasins.

The pay-off came to an abrupt halt. I swept my precious cheques and ink against the wall and got on my feet to face the riot. Marsdon was bellowing orders that nobody heard, and Jordan was shouting in my ear, ". . . save his breath. No room to fight, anyway." He also mentioned something about sardines. I muttered, "They're doing pretty well." The brawl swayed to and fro, a confused mass of shouting, stamping men. The contagion spread quickly to the crowd outside, old camp rivalries springing into instant flame, and little knots of bearded lunatics stamped about in the snow, swinging fists with joyous abandon. They had plenty of room for battle, and this out-door contest became at once an old-fashioned lumberjack scrap, a knock-down-and-drag-out affair with every man a foreman and no holds barred. Inside, Marsdon, Jordan and I remained uneasy spectators of a brawl rendered impotent by sheer lack of elbow room. Fists whirled perilously close to our noses at times, by accident or design, and we were in constant danger of being crushed by the swaying weight of human flesh; but we would comfort ourselves with the reflection that a great deal of animosity against ourselves was now finding outlet in the general eruption.

We did not have this comfort long. The fire, forgotten in the rush of battle, had roared up the chimney and gone out, perishing for lack of fuel. The fact was called to general attention by a gaunt apparition with slightly liquor-glazed eyes and a fiery red beard that straggled in clumps over a long horse face. It leaped upon the stove, rising above the hurly-burly like a jack-in-the-box, and from this vantage began to shout, "Comrades! Comrades!" in a voice of surprising power. It rang over the hubbub like a trumpet call and brought the tumbling mob to a halt. "Comrades," blared the trumpet. "Put down y'fists! Put 'em down. Ain't there struggle enough for the workin' man, 'thout fightin' among y'selves? Fools! Fools! Is this the end o' y'sufferin'? Sweat all Fall fer a few lousy dollars—pay seven'y-fi' cents a day fer grub that ain't fit fer a pig—tramp twen'y-thirty fer y'pay—sleep all night in a barn—wait all day fer a cheque—not hard money, comrades, but a cheque—another piece o' cap't'list paper—n' then bust into a row among y'selves. Fools!" He stabbed a long grubby finger over their heads toward our little silent group. "There! There stands the represen' tives o' Cap'tal. Laughin' up their sleeve—an' well they might!" He continued in this strain at some length, calling them the 'proletarry' and trumpeting of the 'classes' and the 'rights of Man.'

It was strange talk for that modest little shack at Duncan's. The name of this backwoods Lenin (Marsdon whispered to me) was M'Phee. A product of the Sydney coke-ovens, born in a stewing wooden tenement within bottle-throw of Whitney Pier, where the human dross of the steel industry forms a cosmopolitan eddy of black, brown and white, and where the air is thick with soot and sin and labour politics. The politics of this brassy-voiced Gael were as red as his whiskers. He was eloquent, too, in a wild on-to-the-Bastille fashion. The men began to cheer him at each pause for breath. There were cries of "Yay! You tell 'em, Mac!" Some wag evolved a couplet on the spur of the moment, which they chanted in wild chorus—

"Dollar'n a half a cord,
An' seven'y-fi' cents board!"

By this time the orator had worked them to a fine pitch of excitement, the spirit of revolution was in the air and I began to wonder vaguely about the outcome. *A la lanterne?* The Seine? The guillotine? But there was not a lamp-post in Duncan's Corner; there was a foot of ice on the lake behind the village; and the only guillotine in Pine County was that decrepit affair in George Barrish's printing shop.

As usual, it was the unexpected that happened. The apostle of revolt made an astounding dive into his shouting audience. It was a thing of magic, a trick of disappearance worthy of Houdini himself. At one moment he was there, perched on the rusty stove, waving his ragged arms and trumpeting like an enraged elephant, and then in a trice he had vanished. There was another great convulsion in the mob, and the sounds of combat broke out afresh. Afterwards I knew that some joker had so far forgotten the rights of man as to slip a strong hand through the edge of the audience and pull the orator's feet from under him in a single expert twitch. The position of that swaying human volcano had been a tempting one. But at the time I could only be concerned over this new turn of events, and its transition from hot words back to open warfare. Until now I had hoped that we might demand the right to be heard, snatching a fortuitous moment from the armistice that the Trumpet had secured, and pointing out that they might as well get their pay first and fight afterwards. There were sober men among them, I knew, who would back me up in this. But these great expectations had gone down to the plank floor with the miserable man from Sydney. Once more the little shack became a whirlpool of brawling men, in which the orator vanished as a drowning chip.

Someone had said, early in the riot, something about a knife. The unwelcome memory emerged from the background of my thoughts and began to loom unpleasantly. All the foreigners carried knives. So did some of our own woodsmen. If someone "drew his side-arm clear" Duncan's is three thousand miles from Silver Street, and this was no mere tussle of soldiery out for a lark. If someone drew his side-arm clear there would be blood on the moon and no stopping when the first man dropped. Through the ragged porthole of the broken window-pane I could see old Jacob Parrel peering from the door-way of his store across the street. The lower part of his small plate-glass was a white half-moon of frost, but I could see the striped sticks of sugar-candy dangling from a string, the bells of crinkled red tissue and a brave glimpse of tinsel and toys. Another string supported a message, printed on bits of coloured paper that swayed like so many poplar leaves from some current of warm air within. PEACE ON EARTH, capered the little papers, GOOD WILL TO MEN. I glanced at the watchful store-keeper, wondering if he sensed the irony of that pirouetting benison, but his face held only vague alarm. He was fearful for the virginity of his window glass, the musty men, and wondering what the world was coming to.

As a matter of fact, it was coming to the third and final act of our merry little farce. The last act, like the second, was opened by a voice crying in the wilderness. Not the Trumpet this time. (That Voice was huddled in a corner, stupid from raw liquor and trampling feet.) Above the tumult rose a shrill voice of "Mind my fiddle! Mind my fiddle!" which was taken up by many voices. "Mind the fiddle!" "Mind Jimmie's fiddle, you!" "Hey! It's Jimmie the Fiddler. Mind his fiddle!" The battle within, doomed to impotency by the lack of fighting room, died away in a ripple of minor hustling. The warriors in the snow outside came in a milling rush to the doorway, eager to know the new excitement. The men in the room, pressed back, created an open space in the floor centre at the cost of oppressed ribs and wall boards. It was plain that Jimmie the Fiddler was a person of consequence.

From the tiptoe of my larrigans I considered him: a short grey wisp of a man with gnarled hands and rather bleared blue eyes. He might have been sixty perhaps. Jordan whispered, rather dramatically, "The Last of the Chanty Men," which made me cock my brows. The picture of our huskies felling trees with a "Way-ay, roll an' go!" was an interesting one. "Old sailor," rumbled Marsdon in my ear. "Quit the sea years ago; been driftin' from camp to camp ever since. Usually hires on as a cookee. Peelin' spuds an' playin' flunkey to the bull-cooks. But it's the fiddle gets him a job. Music in the camp, see? Sing-songs, an' all that." The Fiddler still clutched his instrument, swathed in soiled red flannel, against his skinny breast in a gesture absurdly maternal. His shrunken features were expressionless, a grey stubbled mask in which the watery eyes revolved like those of a doll. Jordan's ear was close. "Now's a chance to do his stuff," I murmured, with all the irony I could muster. "Music hath charm, you know." Jimmie the Fiddler was too far away to hear me; I can swear to that—but fact remains that he took up the challenge. Perhaps he wanted to get his pay and be gone. More likely, finding himself in the midst of a sudden audience, he tucked the worn old violin under this chin from sheer instinct. He poised his bow above the strings in the dramatic gesture of all fiddlers, great and small, and I wondered what the tune would be. Something soft and dreamy, for choice; to remind them of home sweet home and set them fumbling for their cheques amid a flood of maudlin tears. "Mother Machree," perhaps, or "Old Folks at Home." (And, ah for a Kreisler playing an old refrain!) Down swept the Fiddler's bow, shattering the heavy-breathing silence with a wail of strings. The tune was "Shenandoah."

"Shenandoah!" A travesty, that the loveliest of seachanties should be played in a backwoods shack, and by a bleary old cookee whose gnarled fingers writhed over the strings like gnomes dancing on telegraph wires. Yet, after a few bars it became apparent that Jimmie the Fiddler could play, and play fairly well. This was our first surprise. The second came when the bow halted in mid-stroke and he shouted in a high quaver, "Sing! Sing, you lubbers!" Miraculously, someone with a good baritone began, "O Shanadore, I long ter see yew," and twenty voices roared in, "A-way, yew rollin' river!" Away they went with it, the Fiddler swaying from his hips and making a grotesque curtsey as the signal for each chorus.

Now, "Shenandoah" is hardly a song of the lumber camp. Nor is "Rio Grande," or "Blow the Man Down." The sailors among them were steamer men, firemen from the coasting tramps, deck-hands from the laid-up Government fleet, who didn't know a buntline from a capstan bar or a chanty from the Anvil Chorus. Had the Last of the Chanty Men been teaching them the songs of his youth? If so, he had taught them thoroughly, for they went on from—

> "O Stormie's gone, that good ol' man,
> Aye, aye, aye, Mister Storm-along."

to the "Dead Horse," and then to "Hangin' Johnnie" and "Leave 'er, Johnnie, leave 'er." And when the many lines of "Boun' to Alabama" were exhausted, they roared on with "Reuben Ranzo" and "Pay Paddy Doyle for 'is Boots" and "Tom's Gone to Hilo." The Fiddler kept them at it, and when at last they had exhausted his salty repertoire, the bearded chorus was "jes' gittin' tuned up good." The miracle was complete.

Someone now stuck up a real song of the camps, "The Jam on Gerry's Rock." The singer was a young husky with a curly black beard and large dark eyes, the soft eyes of a woman, strange in that rugged frame. His song was a classic of the stream-drivers, the sad and heroic ballad of "Our foreman, Young Munro," and his fatal attempt to clear a log-jam on some long-forgotten river. A simple tune that hovered over a few notes of the scale, and words that by any sophist standard were mere doggerel, but sung by this troubadour with the prize-fighter shoulders and the face of a sombre Christ it achieved a strange and haunting dignity. They heard him to the end in a respectful silence. Your lumberjack is partial to the melancholy. It was an easy step to a dirge more modern—

> "O, they cut down the ol' pine tree,
> An' they hauled it away tew the mill,
> To make a cawfin o' pine

For that sweetheart o' mine,
O' they cut down the ol' pine tree."

There was a rebound from these deeps. Voices were heard calling
upon 'Frenchie' for a song, and some wanderer from the woods of
Quebec began the lively "Alouette," song of the French-Canadian
lumber camps, known and sung from Halifax to Vancouver by French
and other Canadians.

(Solo) "Alouet-te, gentille
alouet-te,
Alouet-te, je te plumerai!
Je te plumerai la tete———
(Chorus) Je te plumerai la tete!
(Solo) Et la tete!
(Chorus) Et la tete!
(Solo) Alouette!
(Chorus) Alouette! O-o-o-o-o-oh!
Alouet-te, gentille
alouet-te,
Alouet-te, je te plumerai!"

They chanted many verses, each verse longer than the one before,
as the unfortunate lark was stripped of plumage on 'bec,' 'nez,' 'dos,'
'pattes,' 'cou' and what not. The sprightly piece, in such sharp contrast
with the mournful favourites of the Anglo-Saxons, and with alternate
solo and chorus like his own beloved chanties, was more to the liking
of Jimmie the Fiddler. With that animation he sawed the old violin,
ducked his head, swayed his shoulders and stamped his moccasined
feet!
    Frenchie held the floor. With a chorus of Acadians from our own
French shore he swung into "En Roulant, Ma Boule, Roulant," canoe
song of the *voyageurs*, of the *coureurs des bois*, the rollicking Gallic
trappers and woodsmen. It had in it the dip of paddles, the swing of
sturdy shoulders, the ripple of northern streams. Men sang and
hummed and whistled it.

The Trumpet had gained his feet. I could see him, stony-faced, in a corner beyond the singers. The rights of man had brought him nothing but a headache. The proletariat were united at last, but in song: song of sea labour, song of woods labour, song of useful men who did useful things, with a pride and joy in the doing. Nothing of the class warfare, nothing of the tyranny of capital. Nothing red in the whole crowded room but his own whiskers and the Fiddler's flannel rag. His eyes met mine in a bleak stare, without hate, but with a quaint gleam of amazed unbelief. Defeat at the hands of the brute forces of Cap't'lism he might have understood, such as a regiment of fur-capped Mounted Police marching in fours up the village street. But a French song and a fiddle!

Men began to drift through the singers, bringing due-bills for payment. Quietly (as one fearing to break a spell) I resumed the crazy chair, face towards the broken window, and spread my cheques and blotters. Somewhere to the right, as an under-current to the bellowing song, came the low rumble of Marsdon, explaining items of account. The fire in the rusty stove was dead long since, and frost of a raw December day came into the shack through every chink and cranny. Gusts of keen wind howled along the street, blowing particles of fine snow through the gaping window, so that it overlay the shelf and papers in a white dust. My bare hands turned senseless, fingers curled about the pen in a frozen cramp. I blew on them at intervals, but the warm breath only awakened a gnawing pain in the knuckles, and at last I abandoned them to the cold. They became a mechanical thing, of a piece with the pen. My Khaki-flannel shirt and light hunting-jacket were as nothing in that knife-like atmosphere, and my feet in the knee-high larrigans seemed mere lumps of cold clay, in spite of thick felt inner soles and two pairs of heavy woollen socks. Bitterly I regretted the mackinaw flung so hastily aside. There were neither time nor room in that gathering stream of men to put it on again.

Men passed behind me in a slow shuffling river, seen only as a succession of work-bitten hands, stained black with dried balsam, which flipped due-bills in payment over my left. They hummed and sang the current song as they shuffled past, and said "Thankee," "T'anks" and even "Thank y', *sir*." By this you may measure the Fiddler's miracle.

A ballad singer took the floor again, a Scot from Pictou way, or some glen beside the Cape Breton lakes, and sang "Lord Thomas and Fair Elinor." The audience clamoured for more, and he gave them "Little Musgrave" (rendered "Muthagrove") and "Barbara Allen" ("as Barbara Ellen")—ballads old as the hills. There followed a brief silence, and then the Fiddler's bow crashed down again with "Workin' on the Railroad," song of the construction camps and section gangs—

"Now we're workin' on the railroad,
    All the livelong day,
Now we're workin' on the railroad,
    Jest to pass the time away.
Can't ya hear the whistle blowin',
    —Rise up so early in the morn?
Can't ya hear the Cap'n shoutin',
    Dinah, blow your horn!"

Frenchie and his chorus followed promptly with another canoe song, "C'est l'Aviron Qui Nous Mene En Haut," and followed it with popular "Malbrouck." Malbrouck, rollicking gibe at the great Marlborough, brought to Canada by Frontenac's solders—

"Malbrouck s'en va-t-en guer-re,
    Mironton, Mironton, Mirontai-ne
Malbrouch s'en va-t-en guer-re,
    Ne sais quand reviendra."

The tune is, of course, practically the same as that of "For he's a Jolly Good Fellow" and "We Won't Go Home Till Morning"; and two hundred voices took it up, singing all three at the same time, each faction trying to shout the other down in a good-humoured vocal riot. A musical comedy manager would have called this the Grand Finale, for it marked the climax of our little play at Duncan's. The "Won't Go Home Till Morning" faction gained headway, was joined by deserters from "Jolly Good Fellow" and finally shouted down "Malbrouch" altogether. They began to troop out into the street, singing lustily, and it dawned on me that I had not written a cheque in fully ten minutes. I turned in the hard chair to find fifteen men singing in a group about the Fiddler and the rest wandering along the street towards M'Kenzie's Garage and Livery Service. Marsdon was stuffing papers into his haversack. "I guess that's the lot," he said.

Outside, there was a spluttering roar of cold motor engines being started and warmed. Trucks were waiting at M'Kenzie's Garage to convey the men to New Germany, whence the railway ran to the outside world. Crude tents of boards and canvas hung over the truck bodies to shelter their human freight from the keen wind, and the floors were deep in straw. Jimmie the Fiddler gave me a nod and a snag-toothed grin, swept a handful of Copenhagen snuff into his mouth and began to wrap the violin carefully in red flannel. The nod said,"That's that!" as of a good job well done; and the grin said, "What'd ye ha' done without Jimmie the Fiddler?" as plain as English. I handed the Fiddler his wages, a cheque for some meagre amount that I cannot remember now, and slipped a five-dollar bill into his hand as well. "Buy yourself something for Christmas," I said. "None of that rot-gut, mind!"

He gave a sort of pull at the front of his frayed woollen cap, with a hand bleached and shiny-clammy from too many immersions in scalding dishwater. It might have been an acknowledgement, a ghost of a salute perhaps, but I think it was simply a part of his process of hitching together for the long cold drive. The fiddle was in a small stained sea-bag on his back, bow-tip and flannel-swatched neck protruding. He pulled on a pair of enormous white mittens and stepped out into the trampled snow of the street. "One moment," I called. "As a matter of curiosity, Jimmie, where did you get those chanties? Been giving lessons?"

The Fiddler rolled the wad of snuff in his cheek and stared at his feet. One moccasin began to trace shapeless patterns in the snow. "Singin' lessons, mister?" He spat a brown stream. "I'm no music-master." The mere thought seemed to anger him. He threw up his head with a rush of words. "Where did the Frenchmen get 'Alouette'? Where did the O'Bretoner get 'Little Muthagrove'? Where else but in their cradles? Where did they get the chanties? Have ye forgot there was a time when this Nova Scotia province was a small nation o' sailors, an' not so long ago? But that was before the war, before your time, I guess. Kruger's war, I mean. Aye, a nation o' sailors; wi' a sawmill on every crick, an' the hearty Bluenose men buildin' their ships an' sailin' 'em over the globe. Bluenose ships an' Bluenose men in every port atween Halifax and Vancouver, *round by the east*. Aye, they called us the hardcase Bluenoses, when the tall wind-ships flew about the world, because we were hard drivers, an' feared nothin' this side of Judgement Day. But that's all done an' gone, now. The steamboats drove us off the sea, our wind-ships an' our chanty songs as well, for your sea-goin' mechanic does his work to numbers an' a jangle o' bells. He wiped out the snow pattern with a sweep of his foot. 'The fathers an' gran'fathers o' these lumberjacks were sailors, mister, most of 'em, with a job for every minute an' a song for every job. That's where your huskies got the chanties. You can rock a cradle to 'Reuben Ranzo'—did ye know?—an' saw firewood in the door-yard to 'Leave 'er, Johnnie.' "

He spat again, and wiped his stained lips with a sleeve. "Now we're cuttin' down our fine tall spruce an' makin' it into paper, 'stead o' buildin' ships. Papers for the scurryin; city people, who only care for the ink that's on it an' nothin' at all for the wood that's in it. Aye, good ship-wood blowin' about on windy corners in the dirty city streets. That's what we've come to, mister. That, an' this damned radio riggin' on every farmhouse, an' the kids learnin' nigger music an' the whinin' songs o' cattle-drivers." The Last of the Chanty Men turned abruptly, wriggled the pack into a more comfortable berth between his bony shoulders, and trampled away. There was a single farewell flourish of white mitten as he clambered into the waiting truck.

Marsdon came out of the deserted shack, blowing on his fingers and squinting his eyes against the blinding light of the street.

"Who's that?" he rumbled, without curiosity. I watched the truck move off.

"Orpheus," I said. Marsdon grunted and ran over a mental list of names without success.

"Must be a feller from Camp Four," he said.

The Lower Learning

It was typical of Milt Foster that he bore no resentment towards the two young men. "I don't want you to think," Young Arnold had said, "that I haven't the same confidence in you my father had. Why, Milt, you're a Kempenfelt institution. It's just that times have changed and we've got to consider new ideas. The Kempenfelt lands have been logged flat. For years now we've had to pick up odd lots of timber wherever the logging chances were good and the price was right. On the whole, your estimates have served very well; if some fell short on the actual cut, there were others that over-ran. You understand, I'm saying nothing against the old methods of timber-cruising. But here in Nova Scotia timber's getting scarce and the price goes up every year. We've got to put our timber-buying on a scientific basis. We must know what's there and where it lies; the grades on the hills, the nature of the swamps, the length of the hauls, the economical location for each camp, the possibilities of the streams for *driving*. We *must know* all these things to a mathematical point. We've got to take the uncertainty out of the logging business."

"I see," Milt said mildly, wondering how all this was to be accomplished.

"I knew you would," Young Arnold continued. "Of course, we're only a small concern and we can't afford to hire an up-to-date man with experience, but I'm getting a couple of young forestry students from one of the universities to come down and tackle a problem or two. They'll be glad of a summer's work at a hundred a month apiece, and right now I've got a proposition they can whet their teeth on. I want you to go along, learn what you can from them, and make an independent report."

Milt, whose pay for years had been ninety dollars a month, was surprised at the light way Young Arnold spoke of a hundred. The firm had been cautious about wages. Old Mr. Kempenfelt always conveyed an impression that his business tottered on the verge of bankruptcy, and Milton Foster's loyalty forbade the view held by the village cynics, who suggested that three hard-headed generations of Kempenfelts had garnered a tidy family *fortune.* Now old Kempenfelt was dead and Young Arnold, thirty-five and full of repressed ideas, was injecting some new life into the business. There had been repairs to the dam, efficient new water-wheels, and an up-to-date accounting system that sent old Martinside, the head book-keeper, into a shocked retirement. And now, inspired by a magazine article on the modern science of forestry, he had cast a critical eye on the fountain-head of the business, the purchase of stumpage itself.

The embryo forest engineers proved to be healthy young men, alert and fluent in discussion of their work and bubbling over with animal spirits the rest of the time. They slapped Milt on the back, called him Old Timer with comradely patronage, and gave him a trick cigar that exploded with a shocking bang and scattered sparks all over the village barber shop. Milt took it all in good part. It was impossible not to like this pair of hilarious children just released from the grind of a college term, although he wondered if, in refusing to take life seriously, they were approaching the serious business of timber-cruising in anything like the proper spirit. Ryerson was tall and rangy, with large innocent blue eyes and the bland manner. His face was tight-drawn and of the wax-like pallor, impervious to sun, that sometimes goes with athletics.

Barton was small and dapper, pink and brown. In deference to college mode they wore no headgear, rain or shine, parted their hair in the middle, and cultivated moustaches of a prescribed size and shape. With these exceptions they were careless of all appearances, especially in the matter of clothes.

Milt hired a pair of compass men in the village, and a cook named Artemus Bibby, a pale plump man of forty, with blue shaven jaws, and a reputation for being 'cleaner than soap,' and they set out on a cold May morning under grey skies, with a bleak wind in their faces. There were three canoes, The students took one, and Milt and the cook paddled the third. It was a stiff paddle, up-stream and against the wind. Milt let the compass men take the load in their light sixteen-footer. He and the cook brought up the rear where Milt could keep an eye on the students. This was needless. The young men seemed quite at home in a canoe, although on the first portage they had to be shown how to carry one.

"A canoe," Milt explained, "is a thing one man carries better'n two." He showed the trick of turning the canoe on its side, thrusting a knee against the bottom as a fulcrum, and throwing the craft upon the shoulders by a quick heave on the middle thwart. "You got to heave, straighten up, an' turn to catch the gun'les, all in one motion," he said. He demonstrated.

"I didn't get it," Barton said quickly.

"Nor I," say Ryerson.

Milt did it again. As the gunwales settled on his shoulders his voice came with a sepulchral rumble from within the hull. "You got to forgit it's a canoe, see? You got to let on that middle thwart's jest an exter heavy axe you're puttin' on your shoulder; then turn quick an' grab the gun'les." He set the thing down with a grunt.

" 'Fraid we're stupid." Ryerson was apologetic. "Would you mind . . .?"

Milt demonstrated again. In all he swung the canoe on and off his shoulders nine times. He was sweating and breathing hard. It was a violent exercise.

"Give a heave yourself, now," he puffed. "You'll never learn without tryin'."

Ryerson tipped the canoe bottom against his knee, seized the thwart, and threw the craft upon his lean shoulders with practised ease. He stooped carefully and picked up the paddles one by one, sliding the broad blades between himself and the pressing thwart so that they took the weight of his burden and spread it evenly across his shoulders, and then moved off along the portage with a steady step.

"It's wonderful, the things you learn," little Barton said innocently. He slipped a heavy pack-sack on his back, adjusted the tump-line, and followed the bobbing canoe. Like a sunset spread the dull brick flush over Milton Foster's face.

The river-banks were a bristle of hard-hack bushes, the buds just breaking into leaf, and swamp maples leaned over them and scattered bright scarlet blossoms on the water. Sometimes there was a clearing occupied by a tumble-down lumber camp and two or three porcupines squatting in the fitful sunshine, and once the blight of an old forest fire ran back over the hillside like a healed scalp wound. The timber on the river-slopes was scattered and poor, most of its valueless maple and wire birch. The students discussed these things in book terms unknown to Milt. It astonished him to see how quickly they could drop their sportive mood and plunge into earnest debate about 'excessive exploitation,' 'soil denudation,' and the 'effect of timber depletion on stream run-off.' In impressive and mysterious words they condemned the manner in which the watershed had been ravished, an opinion Milt shared, though in simpler language; it seemed fruitless to tell them that logging companies had cut ruthlessly over the protests of the more far-sighted timber-cruisers, who knew full well that the forest was not inexhaustible. The apostles of timber science looked upon the stripped ridges with wise young eyes, and old Milt Foster felt vaguely uncomfortable, as if he were personally responsible for his generation.

They passed through two lakes, and at dusk came to a stream hurtling into the river from the shadows of the west ridge. Its water was yellow and streaked with froth, and it filled the evening hush with the brawl of a long and steep descent.

"MacGowan's Brook," Milt said. "Our job's up there. We'll camp right here. There'll be the devil's own portage in the mornin'." They pulled out the map after supper and spread it before the fire. Milt ran a calloused finger up the brook to a small lake at the head of it. "Somewheres west o' the lake. A two-thousand-acre lot belongin' to the ol' Brantford Estate. Prob'ly take some findin'. Nobody's looked at the boundaries since Simon Brantford blazed 'em a hundred years ago."

"Why should the lot be hard to find?" demanded Ryerson. It seemed very plain on the map.

"It's a long story an' complicated," Milt sighed. "The land titles an' boundaries west o' the river are a mess. It's the ol' Clinton Township, which was named after a General in the American War an' granted by the Crown to a bunch o' discharged soldiers, Highlanders most of 'em, in 1783. This map—it's a copy from the Crown Lands Office—shows the way she was divided. See—Private Neil Chisholm—Private James Chisholm—an' all these MacGowans—half a reg'ment o' MacGowans. That's why the stream's called MacGowan's Brook. Well, the land was forty mile from anywheres an' too stony fer farmin', an' the timber was only a noosance, so after locatin' their grants they just simply packed off to another province, got lands granted there, an' fergot about Clinton Township as quick as they could. It happened frequent in those times. The Crown Land officials, havin' granted it, stuck a map o' the township an' its 'location lands' in a hole somewheres an' fergot about it too. Timber land was cheaper'n dirt those times. You could farm dirt, but you couldn't grow even a Bluenose pertater in land that was half rock an' half pine stumps."

"Then how," demanded Barton, "did the present owners get title?"

"Title? Well, along in the eighteen-thirties the lumber trade begun to boom an' timber lands got valuable all of a sudden. There was a rush to take up all ungranted Crown Lands, an' after that it was a case of buyin' at increasin' prices from people who'd seen what was goin' to happen. Right away, somebody thought o' the Clinton Township. The original grantees an' their heirs couldn't be traced, exceptin' one. They found a feller named Moses MacGowan who could trace hisself back to one o' the soldier grantees—he wasn't real sure which one. So they offered to pay fer quit-claim deeds. Moses done a flourishin' business fer years, peddlin' quit-claims right an' left. That was a hundred year ago. All the present titles go back to them quit-claims fer a jumpin'-off place. I heard a young lawyer say the titles were 'valid only in Mosaic Law.' Anyway, they're a mess from the start."

"You say the boundaries are a mess as well," Ryerson said. "Why?"

"I'm coming to that. When they'd got their quit-claims there was another scramble, this time to locate the grants on the ground. The blazin' had growed over an' disappeared along the lines, an' no corners could be found. Them ol' soldiers had taken a tree at each corner an' blazed it four-square; natur'ly the tree died an' rotted away. But them eighteen-thirty fellers didn't worry much about that; it gave 'em latitude, 'y might say. They jest turned to an' run off the lots accordin' to fancy; if the surveyor spotted a good clump o' timber a bit to the side o' his proper course, he jest natur'ly shifted his course to take it in. An' since the title wasn't none too good to start with, an' the new lines sometimes took in a thousand acres on a grant that was five hundred accordin' to the Crown Land books, they cut off the lumber in a hurry. A late arrival was apt to find half his lot inside another feller's lines an' cut clean; an' with the timber gone, 'twasn't worth fightin' about. Not on a quit-claim deed. So them fancy lines stood, an' after a time the Crown give up tryin' to put the puzzle together an' recognised the lines on the ground."

"It's second growth, then," Barton murmured, disappointed. "I thought we were going to cruise some virgin stuff."

Milt nodded. "You got to remember them eighteen-thirty fellers were after white pine, an' the biggest stuff at that. They wouldn't bother with anything they could git their arms around; they took some spruce, too; but they reckoned the hemlock, the Norway pine, and o' course the hardwood, as worthless. That was a hundred year ago, see? There's a stand o' virgin hemlock on some o' them ol' grants today, an' the pine has growed to a pretty good size ag'in. The spruce was hardly touched. That's what makes it interestin' to the Kempenfelt Timber Company. We been buyin' an' cuttin' these ol' grants fer years, but the Clinton Township still contains some o' the best wood on the watershed. This here lot jest come on the market. Some Halifax lawyers was windin' up the Brantford Estate an' discovered the deed. They sent a feller in to look at the lot. He couldn't find the boundaries—the lines have gone ag'in, and he was a stranger like you boys—but he went back an' reported a good mixed stand along the west shore o' the lake; so they decided to put a price of $30,000 on Brantford's two thousand acres, an' let the buyer find it if he could. That's where we come in. Young Arnold Kempenfelt has got an option, but he ain't goin' to buy a pig in a poke."

The students had a detached air. "Interesting," little Barton said. "But out of our field, of course. A cruiser's not supposed to locate boundaries. That's survey work."

"Mebee so," Milt said. "You're thinking o' big companies an' big staffs. In these parts a timber-cruiser's s'posed to do his own title searchin', his own locatin', an' his own surveyin', not to mention keepin' an eye on the loggin' crew when the land's bein' cut."

"Un-huh." Ryerson yawned. "Time to hit the blankets. And by the way, Old Timer, I wish you wouldn't say 'Norway' when you mean red pine. *Pinus Resinosa* is not native to Norway and has nothing to do with Norway."

"So?" Milt pondered the matter seriously. It touched professional pride, as if he had mistaken birch for beech. "Well, I dunno. The mountain ash ain't peculiar to mountains either. I never seen a witch on a witch hazel, an' I've yet to find crabs in a crab-apple. A Norway pine has always been a Norway pine in these parts, an' I guess I'm too old to learn different."

They were early astir. The brook fell down a two-mile slope in a series of irregular steps. There was no trail. The long uphill portage discouraged trappers and hunting parties. The slope was a wilderness of wire birch and hardhack sprouting amongst a great variety of boulders. The cruising party soon found themselves sweating in the raw spring morning. It was heavy work in rough footing, especially with the unwieldy canoes, which had an uncanny fashion of wedging among the trees. At the top, where the brook poured through a rocky lip and began the long cascade to the river, they looked west across a succession of wild meadows. A cold wind stiffened the sweat in their clothes. The stream lay dark and wide in the meadows like a dormant snake. There were three meandering miles of it, easy paddling, and then a mile of faster water where they had to drag the canoes past occasional ledges.

As they entered Bull Moose Lake the land rose on three sides in steep ridges dark with masses of timber. White pine occupied the skyline, marching in procession along the ridgetops like stately women with incongruous little hats tipped rakishly towards the north-east. Farther down came the hemlock in globular masses of feathery branches, then the crowding spruce and fir, with a pale sprinkle of hackmatack, frail child of the swamp, in the bottoms, and a fringe of birch and maple along the shore. It was a sight to kindle a cruiser's eye. The students crowed happily. They vented their joy in a burst of horseplay, flipping water back and forth at each other with their paddles until a gust of the raw wind caught them in a hilarious moment when the canoe upset. It went over with a weary deliberation, as if it were tired of this sort of thing and resolved to make an end to it.

Cautious Milt Foster had entrusted the students with nothing more perishable than the cook-tent and blankets, reserving instruments, provisions, and other important matter to the other canoes. They were all deep laden and the wind made a nasty lop. The compass men turned their canoe towards the floundering jokers, but Milt roared prompt disapproval. He brought his own canoe to the scene. The capsized canoe had filled and righted itself and lay awash with the bow and stern peaks showing and an occasional glimpse of gunwale. The students swam alongside it, whooping to show their unconcern. Milt looked at the canoe. The tent and blankets, swollen with the water, were wedged tightly under the thwarts. "Git aboard her, boys," he advised.

"Eh?" Ryerson said, treading water. "She'll sink. She's floundering now. You'd better get a line out and try to get her ashore. We'll swim for it."

"Shore!" Milt bellowed. "You'd never make it, young feller. That water's next thing to ice." He dropped his voice to a persuasive note. "Git aboard her, boys, as she is. She won't sink far. She'll settle under you till you're shoulder-deep or so. You got to squat there that way, keep yourself steady by paddlin' your hands, till I can dump my load an' come back."

He swung his canoe towards the shore, a good quarter-mile away, and grunted, "Now, Bibby, man dig! Dig! We got to git back afore them boys git fired o' their waterhorse."

The cook thought of his sodden tent and blankets. "Won't do 'em no harm to let their teeth rattle a while."

"Yeah. But I'm scared they'll strike out for shore. They wouldn't git fifty yards in this water. I seen good men go that way."

Returning, they were greeted with blue grins and chattering teeth. The young men were numb and unable to help themselves very much. Milt, wielding control with the stern paddle, was obliged to keep his craft bow-to and leave rescue work to the nervous and unskilful cook, and after one floundering attempt to get little Barton aboard he called a halt. The compass men had dumped their load ashore and were approaching rapidly. He called to them to salvage the canoe, now awash once more, and set off for the shore with Ryerson and Barton clinging to his gunwales.

They camped in a clump of spruce with a slow rain murmuring on the canvas. Milt found a convenient pine stub shattered and burned yellow by lightning, and he turned it into fuel with whistling strokes of the double-bitted camp axe. With a fire roaring and the greasy black pine smoke rolling up into a grey sky they made shift to dry the blankets. The rain set a definite limit to the efficiency of their wringing and steaming. The compass men cut brush in the afternoon and made a mattress running the full width of the sleep-tent, but the temperature was not far above freezing and the night was comfortless. Nobody referred to the accident. The silence was crushing.

Towards dawn the cold drove them forth to make a fire, and the cook rustled an early breakfast. Gradually the sun brightened the tree-tops above the freezing ground mist. By nine o'clock the air shimmered with heat. Milt spread the map. "She ain't much help," he pointed out. "The lake's all out o' shape for one thing. Ol' Simon Brantford ran out the lines in 1837 an' sketched the lake in after he got home. He'd marked his corners on the ground an' any fool could find the lake. The deed says 'Beginnin' on the west shore at a Norway pine squared three sides an' marked with the letters S.B.' We got to find that Norway."

"Red pine," murmured Ryerson.

They scattered along the shore in search of it. The lake was a crude triangle a mile to each side. At the end of the day they had examined every red pine, living or dead, within twenty feet of the west shore, and drawn a blank. There were not many to inspect. The natural habitat was higher up in the gravelly soil of the slope. In the midst of supper Milt put his plate down suddenly.

"Jumping Jehoshaphat!"

"Eh?" demanded Artemus Bibby sensitive about his cooking.

"That ol' stub I cut up fer firewood yest'day. She was a Norway, boys, sure as death. Tell by the pitch. I bet we've burnt up ol' Simon Brantford's corner tree." The amputated stump was just above the beached canoes. They went over to it and hunted for chips and fragments. What they found did not enlighten them. "Tomorrer," Milt said, "we'll hit back from this stump on the compass course."

"What about magnetic variation?" Barton said. "That was a century ago."

"Right! I worked out the declination afore we started. But you'll find in runnin' out these ol' boundaries that the magnetic variation ain't hardly worth considerin'. It's the human variation you got to allow fer. We'll run out the course—an' foller it up, all walkin' abreast an' watchin' fer signs o' the ol' blazin'."

In the morning one of the compass men hooked the end of the survey chain to his belt and started up the slope, compass in hand. Milt stood by the pine stump, watching the steel tape slither in his wake. As it drew towards the end he called, "Chain!" The compass man halted, put a small blaze at the nearest tree, and went on slowly. The party moved off abreast, fifteen feet apart, examining each trunk at about shoulder level. In the thick growth of spruce and fir it was hard going. The compass man plunged faithfully into thickets and over boulders and windfalls. Regularly Milt's sonorous "Chain!" echoed in the still woods. They were glad when the big hemlocks appeared. Undergrowth could not exist in this green gloom. Twice there was a shout and the party gathered to discuss a scarred tree. Milt dismissed the first at a glance. The second he opened with short careful strokes of his axe. He shook his head. "Might a' been done by moose or deer. Porcupine, mebee. Hard to say. It's old, but t'ain't axe work."

At forty chains he called Barton to take his place on the line and moved along to the right. They were in the white pine now, approaching the crest of the first ridge. Where the ground began to drop again he called a halt.

"Go back and try again?" Ryerson suggested. To his fresh mind the whole business was typical of the past and its shiftless methods. He saw Milt Foster as a reincarnation of the ineffective to-hell-with-posterity Simon Brantford. In his faded and battered homburg hat, his patched mackinaw shirt, his shapeless bull's-wool trousers, with his grey-stubbed jaws and puzzled grey eyes, the old cruiser was a picture of ineptitude. He waggled his head slowly. "It's this or nothin', to my mind, boys. Look, now. Where the line topped the ridge it's likely ol' Brantford stopped long enough to put the survey mark—three hacks— in one of his blazes. That wouldn't heal so quick as an or'nary blaze. Scatter along the ridge-top a bit, boys. If it's a livin' tree you got to look fer somethin' queer about the bark.

The hunt spread along the ridge, and after an hour came together reporting no luck. The students plainly considered it a wild-goose chase. In spite of this, or because of it, Milt Foster refused to give up. He had not forgiven himself for burning the possible key to the mystery. He left the sweating group on the compass line and walked slowly to the left, turning here and there to catch the sunlight at various angles on one of the trunks.

"The General," Ryerson murmured, "is going to fight it out on this line if it takes all summer."

They saw him step slowly around a thick white pine bole. He circled it three times, stooping and squinting upward. They sauntered over to him, examined the tree and saw nothing. "Look-a-here," Milt said. "There's two spots on this tree, shoulder level—jest right for a blaze—where the bark looks a mite different. Closer-fibred like. Shiny. You got to catch the sun on 'em the right way. One faces east, the other west, jest the way ol' Brantford'd blaze a tree on the ridge-top." Again, the party stooped, squinted, and were non-committal. Milt took his light single-bitt cruising axe and chopped delicately. The bark came away from the supposed west blaze. The wood revealed not a trace. He widened his cut and chopped steadily towards the heart of the tree, clean white chips falling in a slow rain. At a depth of nine inches he paused, doubtful. He made another diffident stroke or two, and a tiny panel came away whole to reveal a bit of glazed grey surface. They all shouted together. When the old blaze was laid bare entirely they saw in its face the transverse furrows made by three upward strokes of Simon Brantford's axe in 1837. The compass men, who had seen such things before, were nevertheless impressed. The students, who had read but not seen, were astonished. "Made the year Victoria came to the throne," Barton said, "and sealed in the heart of a tree all these years. And we've found it. It's like black magic."

"Luck," said Milt.

"Not to mention horse-sense and a good pair of eyes," Ryerson said handsomely.

With confidence they ran out the remaining sixty chains of the south boundary and found themselves in the edge of a swamp dotted with sickly hackmatack. Milt consulted his note-book. The deed said: '. . . one hundred chains to a pile of stones set upon a boulder.' There was a choice of boulders, rising like islands in the sea of swamp hummocks. None bore a heap of stones. "Fell off," Milt suggested. "Knocked off, mebee, by a moose rubbin' off his velvet. Prob'ly wasn't no more'n a half-dozen small rocks grubbed out o' the edge o' the woods an' balanced on the boulder." They probed in the soggy hummocks. Beside one of the granite boulders Barton found a few chipped hunks of whinstone lying together in the peat and hidden by a mat of swamp grass. There was no other evidence. After a careful look at the whinstone fragments Milt determined to consider the corner found. "Them hunks was broke off another rock somewheres, prob'ly with the back of an axe, an' carried here. Means it was wintertime an' rocks hard to find. An' whinstone cracks easier'n granite." They rummaged the near-by woods for better stones, while Milt cut a post of the rot-resisting hackmatack and hewed it square. With the narrow blade of his jackknife, kept razor sharp for such purpose, he carved a neat S.B. on the sides to face north and east, added his own initials and the year on one of the blank sides, and wedged the post firmly in the cairn. It made an imposing little monument.

From it they measured off the long west boundary, '200 chains to a yellow birch squared two sides and marked S.B.,' and found themselves gazing expectantly at a dense growth of mixed hardwood. "That's a long hitch," Milt said. "Chances are we're wide o' the ol' line, but yaller birch don't appear to be too plentiful hereabouts. If the tree's livin' she ought to show up. Look for a big one." They scattered, and one of the compass men walked sixty steps direct to a stout old monarch, four feet through the butt. Healed wounds were evident under the yellow rags of outer bark. Milt chopped a deep splayed niche to expose the old hewing on the east side. Simon Brantford's 'S.B.,' carved with care in the grey face, was as plain as on the day it was made. Little Barton pointed out where the knife had slipped once or twice on the difficult loops. The students took measurements and notes on the growth over it, and Ryerson fished a camera from his pack and took pictures.

They chained boldly towards the fourth corner, and drew a complete blank. The 'stake marked S.B., set in a split rock' must have mouldered away long since, and boulders split by ages of sun and frost here. Milt sent Ryerson with a compass man back along the course to hunt for signs of the old line blazing. With Barton and the other compass man he set off southward. After describing the missing corner the deed said vaguely, 'thence southerly to the shore of Bull Moose Lake and following the shore of said lake to the place of beginning.' The land here was low, clothed mostly in black spruce, with irregular knolls of pine. After a mile or so the woods opened slightly to the eastward and they caught the flash of water. It was not far to the shore. They followed it back northwards to a small cove, where the lake trended eastward. It seemed the obvious jumping-off place for the boundary line. They moved off due north, and after ten minutes found healed scars on a pair of oaks standing a few feet off the course. Milt's sharp axe exposed the buried blazing. At a mile they halted and made casts on all sides without success. From one of the low knolls Milt looked across a swale and saw Ryerson's red shirt moving along the supposed north boundary. They joined forces. Ryerson had found a blaze, but in the angle of the converging courses there was nothing. Again they scattered, each hot for the honour of discovery. It was not long before one of the compass men uttered a triumphant "Wahoo!" His voice seemed to come from space, from the sky itself. They closed in upon a knoll and found him standing twenty feet about them on a great cube of whinstone, completely masked by a surrounding clump of black spruce. The rock was split neatly down the centre, coming together like a pair of lips at the top and widening towards the plinth of bed-rock on which it stood. They peered down at the littered dung of a porcupine den. "The rock prob'ly showed up like a house in Brantford's time," Milt observed. "The spruce has growed up since." It was a good day's work.

The next was spent in heavy toil, cutting out and blazing the boundaries throughly. They set up a cairn and hewn post on the shore opposite the fateful pine stump, and after some deliberation another under the great yellow birch at the north-west corner of the lot. They laid bare the great split boulder on it south and west sides, slashing the spruce away mercilessly, and with much pains erected a cairn on top. In camp that night the students covered the map with a gridiron of pencil lines, and Milt, fighting off his weariness, took a lesson in scientific timber-cruising.

"We'll do it by the strip method," Ryerson said, in the tone of a schoolmaster. "The forest types vary roughly with the topography, so we'll run our cruise lines across the contours—in this case from west to east—at ten chain intervals. We'll use the west boundary for a base line. As for the actual cruising, Old Timer, we leave nothing to chance. We walk each cruise line behind the compass man, counting all merchantable trees within twelve feet, both sides, and grouping them according to species and diameter."

"What?" Milt blurted, astonished. "That'll mean—lemme see—roughly twenty-five miles o' cruise lines. D'ye mean to say you're goin' to actually count and measure every merchantable tree in a strip twenty-four feet wide an' twenty-five miles long? Oh, boys, you'll be here all summer."

The students smiled at each other across the map. "We'll do just that," Ryerson said patiently, "and it shouldn't take more than four days with two cruisers. Point is, we can judge the small trees, pulpwood size, with the eye. The big trees, too, for that matter, but we put the calipers on 'em frequently for checking purposes."

"What about height?"

"We carry hypsometers for that. Measure a tree of each species for height every twenty chains, and work out a volume table on that basis."

"Sounds like a lot o' work."

"Sure. In addition, we'll map the contours roughly as we go. When we're through, the logging boss can take our map, see where the timber is, where he can put his camps to best advantage, and where his roads should go."

Milt was impressed.

They were up at day dawn, shifting camp to a point on the shore opposite the centre of the lot. Barton took one of the compass men and left for the north-west corner armed with instruments, field-book, tea-pail, and sandwiches. Milt, full of curiosity, followed Ryerson and the second compass man to the cairn in the swamp. They measured off five chains along the west boundary, and Ryerson notched a tree and pencilled a figure in the clean wood. From this point the compass man turned east, dragging the steel tape. "Chain!" Ryerson called. The compass man snapped a twig to mark the point, and Ryerson moved slowly towards him, head turning left to right, counting devotedly, pencil busy in the field-book. He stopped to put his long-jawed wooden calipers on several of the bigger trunks, and once or twice paced off twelve feet to the side, checking the imaginary line of the strip. At the broken twig he paused, and the compass man went east again. When they emerged on the lake, Ryerson measured back to the shore cairn for a check. Then, ten chains past the first cruise line, the compass man swung off towards the west boundary again followed slowly by Ryerson, counting, classifying, measuring, mapping, a picture of busy efficiency. The work was conducted in a silence broken by the regular cry of "Chain!".

They lunched on a sunny rise, surrounded by maples just breaking into leaf. The day was warm. For the first time they were bothered by blackflies.

"Another day like this" Milt observed, "an' they'll be bitin' good."

"We should have brought fly-dope,"Ryerson said. "The cold weather fooled me. We'll be eaten alive if we don't look out." He was anxious. The little black pests were settling on his bare head, burrowing under the hair, clustering hungrily in the shelter behind his ears.

"Better smear your phiz with a pork rind," Milt said, "same as me an' the compass men."

Ryerson looked his disgust. "Too primitive, Old Timer. We'll have to send off for grub at the end of the week. We must remember to get some dope."

In the afternoon Milt left the party to embark on his independent cruise. Like the pork rind his method was primitive. It depended utterly upon a sharp eye and a faithful memory. He followed the general course of the ridges, crossing repeatedly from side to side like a schooner tacking against a head-wind, comparing what he saw with a mental file of timber stands estimated and cut in the past—a Bertillon system drawn from a lifetime of experience. He made notes in a disreputable field-book from time to time, and smoked a charred apple-wood pipe with enjoyment. He liked solitude in the woods. Solitude made you part of them. Voices and the tramp of other feet ruined the peace like an alien invasion. He had the old logger's love for good timber on the stump, a trait always curious to strangers who see the lumberman as a callous butcher of trees, and he moved quietly through this rich stand with an air of reverence. There were not many stands like this nowadays; not in Nova Scotia anyway.

By the evening fire the students compared notes, and for diversion teased Milt about the 'Bush-whack System.' Milt was not to be drawn, so they turned their humour upon Artemus Bibby, a man greatly afraid of bears. They announced a 'clawing tree' not far from the tents, with new claw marks and fresh hair caught in the bark. The new marks were a foot higher than any of the older ones, they said, and they had seen his tracks in the mud. "A foot on him, Bib, like a baseball mitt." They hung the evening with tales of bears, and when Artemus retired and filled the privacy of his cooktent with uneasy snores they took him front and rear, Ryerson reaching under the tend wall to claw with hard-hooked fingers, while little Barton screamed "Bear!" in the doorway. It was an unqualified success. Artemus rose with a single yell and dashed for the door, where a stretched cord took him just below the knees and capsized a bucket of water balanced on the ridge-pole. He came swearing mournfully in his sodden underwear to the door of the sleep-tent, and was answered with virtuous snores; but he took his revenge next day, as camp cooks do, by serving a cold breakfast, a meagre field lunch, and a burnt supper. The righteous suffered meekly with the guilty.

Three days later the students were still hard at work, but Milt was ready to return.

"We want to complete the topographical data for our map of the property," Barton said. "Also we're going to examine the brook thoroughly and report on the work required to fix it for log-driving. We'll be another three days at least."

"We'll need grub," said Artemus Bibby.

"And oil for the lantern," Barton added.

It was agreed that Milt should take the compass men out with him and send them back with supplies. As they pushed off the canoe, Ryerson called out urgently, "And fly-dope, Old Timer. Don't forget it, or we perish."

At the mill Old Timer found Young Arnold inspecting the boiler-house, and they went at once to the office. Milt put his old note-book on the table.

"First, Arnold, take up that option. At $30,000 the lot's a gift. Or mebbe—mebbe you'd prefer to wait fer the young feller's figgers?"

Young Arnold picked up the 'phone and sent a telegram of acceptance without a second's hesitation. It was an unexpected vote of confidence. There was a warm glow in Milt's bosom.

"Here's what I make of it, Arnold. The lot's well wooded all over. There's five million feet o' white pine, nice clear stuff, worth five dollars a thousand on the stump. There's mebbe a million feet o' Norway. The young fellers are figgerin' it fer lumber, but I got that contract fer wharf pilin's in mind; them Norway maybe a little gold mine. Call it four dollars a thousand, though, an' be safe. The hemlock, I guess, is worth more as pulpwood than lumber jest now, though it's a shame to see good saw-logs goin' into pulp. Call it fifteen thousand cords at a dollar a cord. Finally, there's the spruce an' fir. The spruce runs about eighty per cent; some saw-logs, but I figgered it all as pulpwood in view o' the market. Sixteen thousand cords at a dollar'n a half—spruce makin' better pulp than hemlock. Altogether I figger the lot's worth $68,000, present stumpage prices."

"Milt," Young Arnold said, "I owe you an apology. I got thinking about it after you'd gone. Your estimates have always checked out reasonably close to the cut. The modern cruising, no matter how scientific, couldn't make much difference after all. But you saw it in action—what d'you think of it?"

"It's good," Milt said honestly. "I got to admit it. 'Course, they got a lot o' fads, like sayin' 'red pine' every time they see a Norway, an' windin' off long Latin names fer trees an' the bugs that kill 'em; but when it comes to cruisin' they go about it pretty thorough. It's all based on actual count an' measure in test strips. Their figgers are pretty sure to be on the safe side, because a man's more apt to miss a tree than to count one too many; also he's measurin' the width o' that strip with his eye, an' the strip is apt to shrink a bit, 'specially along late in the afternoon, say, when a feller's in a hurry to finish a cruise line. Them boys showed me their figgers for the south end o' the lot—they worked 'em up on that bit for a comparison—an' they come a little under mine. On the whole, I guess we'll check out pretty close."

"Humph. Then what's the good of all this science, Milt?"

"Well, sir, on a lot no bigger'n this I'd say it ain't any better'n the ol' way. But on a real big block their system'll still give a good average where the ol' style timber cruiser'd prob'ly guess wide o' the mark one way or the other. 'Specially if the stand's broke up a bit with swamp an' barren."

Young Arnold stirred and frowned. "There are no big blocks in these parts, Milt."

"No. That's why I still got my reputation. But what I said holds good. I been doin' some thinkin', too, while I was gone. We slep' in wet blankets one night an' I found my bones ain't so waterproof as they used to be. I'm an ol' man, Arnold. I'll have to quit soon. Who'll you put in my place? Timber-cruisin', ol' style, requires a man that's spent his life in the woods, estimatin' stands an' seein' 'em cut. He's got to have an eye like a hawk, a memory like a filin' rack, an' a conscience like a scoldin' wife. D'you know where you can hire such a feller? Nor do I. Timber-cruisin' used to be a aristocracy; now it's died out, like the Brantfords. A feller with them qualifications nowadays goes into pulpwood contractin' an' makes money fer hisself."

"What are you driving at?" demanded Arnold. "Old! You're as sound as a hackmatack post."

"Yeah," the old quip came readily. "An' a post is sound up to the point where it's stuck in the ground. Here's what I'm comin' at. Give me one o' them boys fer a year or two, so I can teach him the things that ain't in books. The local colour, as y' might say. Actual cruisin' he knows. That's science. Science cuts out so much guesswork that you don't have to hire a good guesser any more. But science ain't enough fer a lone cruiser in a small outfit hereabouts. Give one o' them boys the local colour an' he'll do a better job than the best ol' timer that ever blazed a line."

"That means a better job than you," Young Arnold said. "I don't believe it. But there's something in what you say. Where are the boys now?"

"Up at Bull Moose Lake, usin' their education. They're surveyin' for haulin'-roads an' camp locations, an' figgering' on a flume to carry logs down the big hill to the river. Scientific, as y' might say."

"Ah!" Arnold saw the twinkle in the keen old eyes. "And what's the local colour?"

Milt smiled gently. "That lot was logged fer the virgin white pine back in Simon Brantford's time. It was big stuff an' he had to find the easiest grades an' smoothest bottom to haul out to the lake. There was signs of his ol' log landin's on the lake shore, so I traced back the ol' haulin' roads from there. They're all growed up in spruce an' hard-wood thicker'n a boot-brush, but I found 'em with a stone-hammer here an' there, bits o' the ol' cord'roy still existin' under water in the swamp holes—there's a heap o' signs if y' know what to look fer."

"And the brook?"

"She winds through three mile o' wild meadow an' then pours through a break in the rim o' the plateau down to the river. Ol' Brantford jest built a dam acrost the break. It rotted an' disappeared long ago, but you can still see where he butted the sills ag'in the bank. He flooded the meadows five or six foot deep an' backed water clear up to the lake; then he towed his logs in booms from the lake to the dam an' sluiced 'em over. With the exter rush o' storage water under 'em the logs never had a chance to git into trouble."

"You are a great man," Young Arnold said. "How do you do it?"

"Local colour an' usin' my eyes," Milt said simply. "In these parts a cruiser's got to know his local hist'ry, joggerphy, jollogy, an' human nature, an' be a sort o' backwoods detective into the bargain. They don't teach them things in college." He grinned. "I learnt a lot off them boys, though. Outside o' scientific cruisin' I learnt to look sideways at a free seegar, to hunt the frogs out o' my blankets afore turnin' in, to be non-shallant when I found a dead skunk in my hat, to tell the difference 'tween tea an' boiled terbacca, to pick up a tin plate ginger-like— they're hot if they've been stood ag'in the fire when you wasn't lookin'—an' to be awful suspicious when a tent leaks on a fine night. A fine smart pair o' boys, them. Fussy as women about their hair, an' reg'lar dudes with them little mustaches, but clear o' that a re'lar pair of woodsmen an' the best o' comp'ny. We never had a dull moment."

He went off to order supplies. In the village hardware store he demanded canoe varnish. "Somethin'," he said, "that'll dry quick an' set hard."

The clerk swept a can off the shelf. "This here," he declared, "will dry like spit on a hot stove an' set like Portland cement."

Milt went along the street to order groceries, and watched them packed into boxes suited to the canoe and the long portage. Finally, he entered the drug-store and asked for fly-dope. "The best you got, Harry."

Harry stood a labelled bottle upon the show-case with pride. "There you , Milt. Hennigar's Liquid Fly and Mosquito Repeller, Warranted Not to Harm the Most Delicate Skin."

Behind the blacksmith's shop, just above the canoe landing, Milt poured Hennigar's Liquid Repeller over a litter of old iron and refilled the druggist's bottle from the can in his pocket. He thrust home the cork with care. The compass men were stowing groceries in the canoe. "Here's the dope for Barton an' Ryerson," he said casually. "Hennigar's patent. Harmless to smear it on lavish 'specially in the hair. An' give 'em my kind regards."

He watched the canoe out of sight and dropped the guilty can in the river.

Mr. Embury's Hat

Mr. Embury wore his new spring hat, a smart green affair with a little whisk stuck in the band, like the one young Longford had been throwing on the office tree lately. Mr. Embury was glad he had laid aside at last the sedate bowler. This jaunty green thing rejuvenated him. He felt ten years younger.

His companions in the smoking compartment of the 8:15 were quick to notice it. Buxton—Buxton of the Olcott Oil & Lubricants—told him he was looking younger every day. Phelps the lawyer declared he wouldn't have known Mr. Embury at all except for the hair and the walking stick. Jarvis of the Argus Fire Assurance announced his intention to get a hat exactly like it. The thing was a triumph. Mr. Embury had been a little afraid lest it take away some of the dignity which sat upon him so becomingly in the smoking compartment.

Mr. Embury prized this dignity very much. For him the smoking compartment was a stage on which, twice daily, he played the part life had in fact denied him. His fellow commuters knew that his affairs had to do with the big meat-packing plant on the edge of the city, and by an impressive reticence, broken now and again by some sage remark upon the weightier affairs of "our Company," Mr. Embury had led them to believe his position was one of considerable importance.

Everything about him supported this belief; the gleaming black shoes, the pearl-grey spats, the pin-stripe serge trousers edged like swords, the conservative black overcoat with the plush collar with its plain cravat and the lodge tie-pin, the large well-kept hands and their long manicured nails, the mass of long gleaming silver hair that hung almost to his shoulders, the leather brief case with its gilt initials, the silver-headed walking stick.

A business executive of the old school, he got on the 8:15 somewhere well up the line, beyond all the little suburban settlements of the ordinary commuters. Probably had a country estate. One of those keen old gentlemen who simply cannot retire. They looked at him and thought of Confederation and the days of wooden ships and crinolines and Fenian raids.

Now the truth was that Mr. Embury lived in a frowsy boarding-house at Pottsville. He lived there because it was even cheaper than frowsy boardinghouses in the city, and because the expense of railway fare was more than compensated by the pleasure of journeying twice a day with that select little company in the smoking compartment, a gentleman of the old school among his peers of the new. There were no country estates at Pottsville. There was nothing but the big railway repair shops and a surrounding huddle of wooden houses and pool-rooms and grocery stores, with a fringe of down-at-heel farms. Mr. Embury lived cheaply because "our Company" paid him twenty dollars a week. At one time it had been twenty-five, but that was before the Depression and the twenty-five per-cent cut. "Our Company" had given Mr. Embury to understand that he was lucky to have a job at all. After all, he was seventy, and there were plenty of thrusting youngsters eager to work for less than that. Any sixth-grade schoolboy, Mr. Tyrconnel had once told him brutally, could sit at a desk and check invoices.

Mr. Embury did not look his age, hat or no hat. People took him for sixty quite often. He had always dressed well. In his younger days he had been rather fond of the bottle. That was over, of course, except for the single bottle he purchased every Saturday night. With its aid

Mr. Embury spent his Sundays in a delightful realm far removed from Mrs. Brannigan's, although his apparent self lay on a narrow bed behind a locked bedroom door in that tolerant woman's house.

It was a fine morning in May, and from the window of the smoking compartment Mr. Embury surveyed the flickering landscape with enjoyment. The snow had gone, and the cold, and in a very little while now the trees would be in leaf. The weather had been perfect for two weeks; a little rain, Mr. Embury observed aloud, would be very useful, very useful indeed—in just the right tone, the mild, uncomplaining tone of a gentleman-farmer who does not question the workings of divine Providence but likes a just balance between the needs of town and country. As the 8:15 plunged through the pine woods a hot resinous smell entered the compartment windows and battled strangely with the reek of pipe and cigar. The new spring grass had lost its freshness. The air was so hot and still and parched that the passage of the train shook clouds of pollen from the wire-birch catkins along the right-of-way, hanging like thin yellow smoke for a full minute after the 8:15 had passed.

Toward the city the woods were interrupted more and more frequently by clearings full of new suburban dwellings of all shapes and sizes, a painted wooden riot of peaks, turrets, dormers, oriels, gables and sun porches, like the aftermath of a child's game with building blocks. Each group had its flag station beside the railway line, a small red doll's house labelled Leaside, Braemar, Lakeview or Woodvale, where the train ground to a stop and absorbed another quota of smartly dressed men and women bound for the daily toil of an office or shop in the city, all talking in eager, rapid voices of the trout they had caught in the lake last Sunday, or the muskmelons they were setting out, the difference between city and country taxes, and the rising real-estate values of Pinecrest Heights.

In spite of these interruptions the forest extended to the edge of the city, where the meat-packing plant stood like a great brick citadel surrounded by a high fence of steel posts and barbed wire. There the trees rose in a green wave, as if recoiling from the railway track and the brick walls looming beyond, like a sea flung back by a breakwater. Mr. Embury was fond of pointing out that wave.

"Splendid stand of softwood, gentlemen, belonging to our Company. When our people made up their minds to build a new plant, thirty years ago, this site was a mile from the nearest house and three miles from the—um,ah—city proper—in the woods, people said, ha!—and when we moved into our fine new office, B.J.—that's Brace-girdle, our general manager—B.J. pointed out that stand of timber and said to me. 'Embury, my dear fellow, whatever happens we must never cut those trees. They are our lungs, Embury, our lungs. Green lungs, that's what they are. Some day, when the city's grown out to us—as it will, Embury, as it will—we shall be able to turn our faces westward across the railway tracks and breathe the breath of Nature still.' And so it stands today, gentlemen, a visible proof—ha!—that there is senti-ment in business, and poetry behind the executive's desk."

He got off the train as usual at Edgewood, the little red station which now served not merely the meat-packing plant but a flank of the ever-spreading city. From it a spur flowed like a shining steel river through the gateway of the big plant and poured itself over the yard in a delta of little sidings. Employees were arriving at the gate from the city, by bus, car, bicycle and afoot. They called greetings to the watch-man at the gate as they passed inside.

Mr. Embury, with the dignity of the 8:15 smoking compartment still heavy upon him, did not call out "Hey, George! Mornin', George!" like the rest. He inclined the green Tyrolean hat slightly and flourished his walking stick. It was the final act of the morning illusion. From that moment, until the 5:15 picked him up again at Edgewood, Mr. Embury became merely "Hey, Embury!" or "that old fool Embury" to his superiors and "Grampa" to his peers. He had a little desk in a big office. There were twenty other desks, all facing like so many lodestones toward the blank north wall, a vast expanse of painted plaster, unrelieved by window or ornament of any kind. On the other side of that wall was an endless flow of meat in various stages of death and metamorphosis—a scene as remote as China to the occupants of the desks, who could not see through the wall and never ventured to walk around it.

In thirty years Mr. Embury had never been beyond the wall. To the east and south, doors opened upon the offices of department heads and other executives of a calibre large enough to command privacy. Light entered the big room of the small fry through a long skylight, dim with accumulated soot from the plant smokestack, and by win-dows in the west wall, which looked over the roof and skylight of the shipping room to the high brick side of another building. Thus there was no distraction for the twenty-one human moles at their twenty-one oak-veneer desks. It was, as Mr. Tyrconnel frequently pointed out, a place designed strictly for work.

Mr. Tyrconnel was the office manager, and he sat at an opulent glass-topped desk raised upon a dais like a little throne at the back of the big room, where he could watch every movement of the moles. Ten of the desks arranged thus under the godlike eye of Mr. Tyrconnel were occupied by typists, the rest by male clerks. There were half a dozen telephones. All day long the typewriters clacked and the phone bells rang and an office boy ran up and down between the desks, removing and depositing papers that all looked exactly alike. A rushing, noisy place where a side of beef became a cipher on paper, the final metamorphosis.

On the office steps Mr. Embury paused and took a last sniff of B.J.'s green lung. He looked at his watch. He was a full minute early, but he found most of the office staff at work. The morning mail had been sorted and distributed, and the desks were piled high with orders, bills, statements, cost accounts and correspondence. Mr. Tyrconnel was on his throne. He had a silver desk clock, gift from his wife, and he had an uncomfortable way of glancing at it as he lifted his eyes to greet late comers.

Mr. Embury shared a hat-tree with three others. He stood his silver-headed walking stick in the corner by his desk. He removed his topcoat, draped it carefully over a wire hanger, and hung it on the north hook. Finally he took off his hat and placed it carefully, not on the hook, where it might be knocked down by young Longford's carelessness, but on the top of the polished oak tree itself. He disposed of his outer clothing in this manner and in this order every morning and every noon after lunch. It was a ceremony. Young Longford always said Grampa laid his hat on the tree as if he were laying a wreath.

This morning, however, the ceremony halted abruptly just at its climax. "Bless my soul," said Mr. Embury, "Something's burnt my hat."

Miss Partington, who did the Purchasing Department letters, came over from her desk and stared at the hat. "It's a cinder," she pointed out.

It was a cinder about the size of a pea, quite round and very black. It had dropped in the crease of Mr. Embury's fine green hat as a stone drops into a gutter, and it must have been very hot, for it had scorched a large brown patch in the felt before it expired. In fact, even as he felt around for the weak spot inside, his lean finger came right out through it.

Mr. Embury put the hat down carefully on his desk and surveyed cinder and burn in dismay. He felt his ten years come back with a rush. The new hat had cost six carefully-saved dollars. The burn was so plain that he could not think of wearing it on the 8:15 again. No gentleman of the old school could wear a charred hat. As he thought of the train he looked out of the window in a melancholy way. The windows were installed at a height sufficient to prevent anyone at a desk from seeing more than a glass-and-copper skylight and a good deal of brick wall, but if you stood up in the corner beside Mr. Embury's desk, you could see between various buildings, as through an embrasure, a short bit of the railway line, the corner of the Company's steel fence, and a glimpse of the pine and hemlock trees beyond.

And Mr. Embury now saw a wisp of blue smoke hovering over the right-of-way, and a tiny red flicker in the dried bracken just inside the railway fence. He watched it, fascinated, for a moment, saw it creep to the edge of the trees, saw it climb a group of parched firs in a sudden searing rush. Like the puff of an Indian smoke signal a great mass of dun smoke rolled up into the cloudless May sky.

"Fire!" cried Mr. Embury. His high-pitched voice brought the office staff about him in a rush, Mr. Tyrconnel among them, craning to get their heads into the narrow line of view.

"That," said Mr. Tyrconnel, "is Company timber!" He sprang to the nearest telephone and dialed numbers furiously.

In fifteen minutes the Company timber had surrendered itself, tinder-dry, to a great engulfing flame that spread to right and left and sent a volcano of smoke into the sky to join that first magnificent puff. Fire engines came wailing from the direction of the city and were lined at intervals along the highway past Edgewood Station, pouring a collective Niagara into the smoke. The railway rushed out an engine, a tank car of water, and two flat cars laden with section men and fire fighting equipment. The fire crew of the packing plant, amateurs all, and full of amateur zeal, ran hose lines over the tall steel fence and across the railway tracks.

It was all very magnificient and useless. They were simply pouring water upon the black tail of the fire, which was now roaring off into the far-flung bush. It did not stop for three days. The provincial fire-rangers pursued it and harried its flanks with the thin streams from their portable gasoline pumps and the spray of their hand-pumps, but the fire turned and threw them off again, and again as an enraged bull might throw off an attack of yapping puppies. On the third evening rain fell and the fire died. It had consumed ninety square miles of bush and two or three suburban settlements, licking up assorted Swiss, Old English, Cape Cod and Dutch-colonial cottages, bungalows and chalets like an architectural nemesis.

Mr. B.J. Bracegirdle was a very angry man. He did not care about the suburban settlements, nor did he shed tears for the other timber owners, but he sent for the Company lawyer and demanded that a suit be started at once against the railway.

"Of course it was the railway!" he snapped. "The fire broke out a few minutes after the train passed our plant. Everybody knows it was the train."

"Exactly," said the Company lawyer. "Everybody always knows. But nobody ever proves. Funny, isn't it? Look here, B.J., all the evidence you've got is a black desert extending west of the railway line. A casual hobo walking along the track might have thrown down a match. Anything might have happened—it might have started on *your* property and burned down to the railway track for all you can prove to the contrary."

Mr. Bracegirdle considered deeply. There was a grim downward curve at the ends of his powerful mouth. His intensely black eyebrows came together as if for a conference. At last he snapped, "I'm not goin' to let 'em get off without a squeal. You draw up a claim. I'll supply the figures. We'll see what they say."

The railway said nothing for a month. Delay is valuable in forest-fire cases, where obliteration of evidence droppeth with the gentle rain from heaven. At the end of that time they received a violent letter from Mr. Bracegirdle, and judging the moment ripe they sent down a claims-agent to dispose of the matter. He was a stoutish man with greying hair fringing a bald dome, pince-nez, a heavy, drooping mustache, and a double chin. He had a high voice with a curious whining intonation, but there was nothing abject about the rest of him. He was keen and suave and masterful.

In B.J.'s office he read the claim over aloud in such a way that Bracegirdle felt uncomfortably as if he had signed a confession of attempted blackmail. The agent—his name was Preeping—shot the thing to pieces in a five-minute summary that was a masterpiece of polite sarcasm, and finally demanded: "And where are your wintesses, Mr. Bracegirdle? Come now, where are they? Is there a single one?"

B.J. shifted uncomfortably. "Well, there's any number of people saw the fire near the railway fence. There's Miss Partington and—ah—there's Tyrconnel, who sent in the alarm, and—ah—there's old Embury of course. Embury—he saw it first."

He rang for old Embury. Mr. Preeping inspected the old man in a long searching stare. Mr. Embury had once been very tall, but fifty years over an invoice-clerk's desk had bent his shoulders very much. His nose was extraordinarily long. It came straight down his rectangular face and then turned outward in a broad flat tip like the toe of a boot. There were traces of grog blossoms on it still, they had withered in the comparative drought of his later years. His lips were full, the lower somewhat out-thrust, and his cheeks deeply lined. His eyes were calm and grey and very large, with a little fan of wrinkles at the outer corners. Aside from his nose, the really remarkable thing about Mr. Embury was his hair. His brow went up, bald and wrinkled like a parchment, to the top of his skull, where a bushy growth of silver hair began and continued down the sides and back. He had cultivated that flowing white mane ever since in middle age someone told him he looked like Sir John A. Macdonald.

Mr. Bracegirdle tells me you *think* you know something about the fire across the tracks," suggested the agent carefully. Mr. Embury turned his mild eyes to B.J. in enquiry.

"Go ahead!" snapped B.J. "Tell him all you know." It galled Mr. Bracegirdle very much to see how completely the railway man controlled the situation.

"Well, yes," Mr. Embury said. "I saw the fire. It started from the train."

The agent stabbed an accusing finger at him. "How d'you know? Hey? Come! Out with it! You only think so, don't you? D'you realize you may be required to repeat this testimony in court?"

A barrage like this usually fuddled elderly witnesses beyond hope.

"On the contrary," Mr. Embury said, "I am quite sure. I was a passenger on the 8:15 that morning. I remember looking at the exact spot where the fire started, and I can testify there was no fire there then. It was opposite the south corner of the Company's steel fence."

"Where did you sit, Mr. Embury?"

"In the smoking compartment. I always sit there.

"A curious thing, Mr. Embury. The windows of the smoking compartment on that train faced toward the west side of the track—the left side. There's no view to the right at all."

"True," murmured Mr. Embury.

"Now," said Mr. Preeping sharply, "the Company fence is on the right side of the track. You couldn't see it, in other words. All you could see, in fact Mr. Embury, was some timber land, a mass of softwood trees, all exactly alike. Would you mind explaining to me, in simple words that I can understand, how you happened to notice and remember that particular spot—exactly opposite the south corner of the steel fence—a fence you couldn't see?"

"It's quite simple," Mr. Embury said amiably. "The train engineer has to blow his whistle for the highway crossing at Edgewood and he invariably—hum yes—always begins to blow when the engine is abreast of the south corner of the Company's fence. I remember it well. There was a big clump of rhodora, all in bloom, just inside the railway fence. I called it to the attention of my friends."

"Ah! And who were these friends, may I ask?"

"Mr. Embury swelled a little. "Mr. Jarvis of the Argus Fire Assurance Company; Mr. Buxton of the Olcott Oil & Lubricants; and Mr. Phelps, of Phelps, Leavitt, MacInerney and Phelps, the lawyers."

"All very dependable witnesses, no doubt," said the agent irritably. "Go on."

"I got off the train at Edgewood Station. The platform is on the west—that is the left side of the train—so I had to wait for the train to pull out before I could cross the tracks toward the gate of my employers' establishment. There was no wind, exactly, but the air was stirring from the east."

"Why did you notice the wind?"

"The smoke from the train blew along the platform. The line is all up-grade from Lakeview through Edgewood and on into the city, and I know the foreman has to stoke pretty hard on that stretch. I got a bit of soot in my eye, and just after I crossed the tracks something struck my hat. I didn't think anything of it at the time, but when I got in the office I found a coal cinder about the size of a pea in the crease of my new green hat. The felt was badly charred, in fact the hat is ruined, if I may say so—"

"He's not interested in your hat, Embury!" snapped Mr. Bracegirdle.

"Well, as I was saying, I was in the office then, and I happened to look out the window and saw a little wisp of smoke and some flame on the right-of-way."

"Where? Be careful now, Mr. Embury!" Mr. Preeping fixed with a beady black eye.

"Opposite the south corner of our Company's fence. I told you that."

"A most remarkable coincidence, Mr. Embury, don't you think?"

"Miraculous, sir. Miraculous is the word. I could see the clump of rhodora very plainly."

"Humph! Eyesight can be tested, Mr. Embury. You should be cautious. Your office window must be two hundred yards from the railway tracks, and you're an elderly man. Your eyes—"

"Quite, sir, quite. My eyes are very good. So are Miss Partington's. She noticed the bushes, too. The rhodora, sir, has a glorious pale purple bloom which appears in spring before the leaves; one of the natural beauties, sir, of our country-side. A clump in blossom against the dark green background of the pines and hemlocks is a most conspicuous object."

But Mr. Preeping was in no mood for botanical rhapsodies. "Kindly stick to the point, Mr. Embury. You saw this bush from your office very plainly?"

"Yes, sir. Except when the smoke became thick enough to obscure it. You see, the smoke was rising between me and the clump of rhodora."

"In other words," broke in Mr. Bracegirdle triumphantly, "the fire was well inside the railway fence!"

"Please don't interrupt the witness," rapped the claims-agent fiercely. He had seen so many court actions that a court-room manner came naturally.

"There's really nothing more to say," Mr. Embury murmured. "The fire burned through the dead grass and ferns of the right-of-way, and when it reached the edge of the woods it seem to explode in all directions. A remarkable sight, sir."

The agent leaned back in his chair and put his long fingers together. "The gist of your story, then, is this: you found a cinder in your hat and therefore assumed that the train engine was scattering hot particles along the right-of-way. Since the countryside was very dry, such a cinder started the fire. That it?"

"You have put it very concisely, sir. I may add that I can show you the hat and the cinder."

"No doubt, no doubt. There's something you don't know, however, Mr. Embury. All our locomotives are fitted with screens in the smokestack during the summer season."

Mr. Preeping folded his hands and smiled benignly. With his usual acuteness he had gone right to the heart of the matter and stabbed it with a shrewd home thrust. Mr. Bracegirdle slid back into deepest gloom. Mr. Embury stood with his neat hands folded before him. Nobody had asked him to sit down.

"There seems to be something you don't know, too, sir," he suggested gently. "The screens you describe unfortunately affect the draft of the locomotives. The engineers dislike them and the firemen detest them, especially on long up-grades like the 8:15 run. For that reason, sir, the screens are commonly removed, possibly without the knowledge of the management. I don't understand these technical matters very well, I'm afraid; I'm just repeating what the men have told me."

Mr. Preeping's eyes were very wide. So was his mouth. "What men?"

"The mechanics in the roundhouse at Pottsville."

"Pottsville? Absurd! Name me one, Mr. Embury! Name one man in the railway shop at Pottsville who would testify to that in open court!"

"I could name several," Mr. Embury said calmly. "There are three in particular who were laid off last week. Like myself they are—ah—paying guests at the home of Mrs. Birdie Brannigan in Pottsville."

Mr. Preeping put his fingertips together again and blinked his hard black eyes very slowly like a drowsy cat. He was flabbergasted. In all his experience he had never met anything like it. Normally, of course, this concentration of evidence largely would be a weakness to the claimant's case; but when he thought of this calm, unshakable old man in the witness box, with his gentleman-of-the-old-school air, and his fine hands, his tall stooped figure and that noble head—Mr. Preeper shuddered. He turned to Mr. Bracegirdle suavely. "Without admitting a single bit of your man's remarkable story, Mr. Bracegirdle, I'm curious to know what sort of value you put on that burned timber. I must warn you that we've investigated and found your title to that property not all that it should be; and according to reliable evidence most of the burned land was valueless scrub."

B.J. Bracegirdle snorted, but he did not mention the "green lung" of Mr. Embury's 8:15 fancies. "Listen, Preeping! That was a fine stand of spruce, pine and hemlock—a hundred acres such as you wouldn't find anywhere within a hundred miles. I tell you, Preeping, that was our ace-in-the-hole against a sudden shortage in box material. We have our own box factory, see? Buy our logs from farmers and small contractors along the railway. That hundred acres wasn't much, but it'd tide us over an emergency, right alongside our plant, and all. Why, Preeping, that timber was worth seven or eight thousand dollars to us. But I tell you what we'll do. These are hard times for railways the same as anybody else. We'll let you down easy, Preeping. Pay us five thousand and—"

"Ridiculous!" the agent exclaimed. "You know very well you can't prove your timber is worth a cent. Timber's a very uncertain quantity, on the stump. I could quote cases by the dozen. And there's the doubtful title. I'm afraid you're going to have an expensive legal case on your hands, Mr. Bracegirdle. You're going to wish you'd settle for, say, two thousand."

But an unholy light shone in B.J.'s eyes. At last he saw the weapon that lay concealed in the smoke as if it were of the fire. It was not a very ethical weapon. It was not at all the sort of business weapon B.J.

advocated in his frequent speeches to the Boosters' Club; but times were hard, and B.J. was as hard as the times.

"Yeah?" he said, belligerently. "Listen Preeping. You can dispute our title, if you like; you can dispute our figures on the value of our timber. Probably, as you say, we'd wind up with a heavy lawyer's bill on our hands. But we'd have proved, in open court, *the railway's responsibility for the fire!* Think, Preeping, think of those new housing develpments at Lakeview and Woodvale—all those little ugly bungalows and cottages, the pride of the owners' hearts—gone up in smoke—your smoke! Eh? Right now they—and the insurance companies—are out of luck. But if we prove *our* case in court, even though we don't get a cent out of it, the—well, figure it out for yourself."

He sat back in his chair, shrugging eloquently. The claims-agent had been afraid of this, from the moment Old Embury mentioned the fatal cinder. He was a man of decision and he had been given wide powers. He pulled a long typed form from an inner coat pocket and with a smile placed it before B.J. Bracegirdle.

"Sign there, please." He took from his brief case a book of cheque forms marked Special Fund and signed away five thousand dollars with a nonchalance that took Mr. Embury's breath.

"The Company is to be congratulated," said the agent icily, "upon the perspicacity, the memory, the friends, and above all the fortuity, of its servants."

Mr. Bracegirdle, with the cheque in his hands, waving it to dry the ink, looked up at old Embury with wide eyes, as if he had never seen him before. Mr. Embury gave the claims-agent a bow, a queer stiff little bend from the hips, as Sir John Macdonald might have bowed to that fellow Laurier.

B.J. stood up suddenly, clapping him on the shoulder. "Embury! Embury, my dear fellow, you deserve a raise in pay, and by the piper that played before Moses you shall have it! Five dollars a week, Embury, beginning Monday, and the compliments of the management! Ah-ha, don't thank me, Embury, don't thank me at all. The Company has always believed in rewarding faith and—" he paused for a word. Hope and Charity did not seem to be just the thing. "Faith—and fortuity, Embury—in its servants."

B.J.'s thick black eyebrows made triumphal arches in the furrows of his forehead. He beamed. Five thousand dollars, out of smoke—out of thin air, you might say! The timber had been worth fifteen hundred at most. He knew it, the agent knew it, Mr. Embury—but Mr. Embury could think of nothing but this triumph. He closed the General Manager's door behind him quietly and walked through the main office toward his desk with that noble white head in air.

Perspicacity! Memory! Friends! Fortuity! He chewed those magnificient words like cuds. A raise of five dollars a week! He could buy another hat. For that matter he could buy a hat almost every week. Or a quart of government whisky every Saturday night. But he put over the debate, hat versus whisky, to another time. B.J. had called him "my dear fellow"! That was the miracle. In a single stroke all those pleasant fictions of the 8:15 acquired a basis in fact.

Beside his desk he paused, unable in the exaltation of the moment to bring his eyes down to the hateful pile of invoice forms. Instead he gazed out of the window, past the dingy skylight of the shipping room, toward the scene of his achievement. It was blurred a little by the smoke that came rolling down from the tall brick chimney of the packing plant.

Evidently the boiler men were stoking up. Through the open window there came an occasional rattle of hail on the shipping room skylight, and as he watched, a cinder bounced on the sooty glass and came rolling to a little puddle left by the rain in a depression of the flat, tarred roof. It was about the size of a pea. It lay in the edge of the water, hissing for a moment, and then a thin wisp of steam went up and was blown away in the surging smoke.

"Close the window", coughed Miss Partington from her desk. "Close the window, Mr. Embury do! The wind is in the east today."

Swan Dance

Miss Fesant was not beautiful, though she comforted herself sometimes with the notion that her figure was rather good; and she was thirty-five. Her eyes were really her best feature, for she was an incurable romantic and they were large and grey and soft. Her hair was a dead-blond mop which after an application of curling irons looked like a third-rate wig, and her teeth had been repaired by an irregular succession of country dentists. For this reason she cultivated a prim little smile and never laughed. Indeed, after seventeen years of dreary one-room schools and frugal boardinghouses she had ceased to have any desire to laugh. Her parents had been dead many years, and there were no relatives worth mention. She spent her vacations on summer courses at the Normal School, which filled her mind with all sorts of knowledge but did not improve her standing in the eyes of country-school trustees, who believed in reading, writing, arithmetic, and the importance of keeping the tax rate down—in the reverse order of importance.

But at Normal School one year she encountered the passion of her life. There was a course in folk dancing, and Miss Fesant became infused with the spirit of Terpsichore. It was not a passion at first. She thought with the provincial school board that it offered a means of livening the country-school routine. Later, by an ingrowing process, the spirit of the dance became something personal and momentous. She sent for books. Here at last was an emotional outlet that recognized no age in women. Look at Pavlowa! With a growing intoxication she studied pictures of charming females moving birdlike well above the sordid earth, and attended by daringly unclad young men posed in adoring attitues.

She examined her legs and found them long and astonishingly well made. She stood her mirror on the floor against the wall and inspected herself, so to speak, from the spectator's point of view, with a breathless air of discovery. On the strength of this discovery, and to satisfy a craving not yet fully understood; she sent to Montreal for a ballet costume, and when it came she retired to her room and admired herself in the fluffy whiteness for two straight hours. She went on like this, like a female Narcissus with an eighty-by-twelve-inch pool, for several weeks, and from posing she went to the real thing, with "Ballet, in Fourteen Simple Lessons" lying open on the bed. This brought trouble. Unimaginative landladies knocked on her door and asked, "Is anything wrong?" and later told the school trustees that Miss Fesant was subject to fits. And when her leapings dislodged a square yard of plaster from the ceiling of one sacrosanct parlor an outraged woman demanded and secured the dismissal of the schoolma'am on the grounds of secret drinking.

In other places her efforts to teach folk dancing in the village school brought other trouble. It was regarded as a waste of time, and therefore, taxes. In some sections dancing was held immoral, and at the term's end she received a polite farewell and no invitation to return in the fall. Spring—season of joy, especially for young and more personable schoolma'ams—spring was the season of dread for Miss Fesant, a time of waiting, of anxious smiles and secret tears, of an invitation that did not come, a silence that stabbed like a sword. But she persisted in her teachings. In the widely scattered sections of her pilgrimage children learned for a single season how to dance Christ-church Bells, Brighton Camp, Gathering Peascods, Rufty Tufty, Haste to the Wedding and Bonnets So Blue, cultivating "(a) Grace of manner and dignified behavior between sexes, and (b) the art of moving easily and naturally, always maintaining a fair presence and courtly bearing," in the formula laid down by the Normal School.

At last, by a process of gravitation familiar to the sorrowful sisterhood of fading country schoolma'ams, she came to Duffy's Siding, a poor section squatting in the backwoods beside a railway branch line where trains ran twice a week. It had no attraction for teachers who were young, comely, clever and everything else that Miss Fesant was not, so the trustees engaged her and, what is more, kept her. The salary was small, paid if-as-and-when the tax collector could raise the money. Out of her pittance Miss Fesant paid board and lodging, sent to mail-order firms for clothes, looked after personal expenses, and endeavored to put aside something to tide her over the summer vacation and provide for her old age.

The Siding looked for its living to a small lumber mill operating about seven months in the year, and eked out an existence with vegetable patches cultivated in the thin soil of the clearings. A village of morose people living furtively in small unpainted houses as if in beleaguered towers. Once a week the thin clang of the church bell proclaimed a truce in this visible war. They ventured forth and sat, stiff-backed, in hard narrow pews; and a quavering old man told them the meek should inherit the earth, and blessed were the poor—and if the poor did not shingle the parsonage roof next fall, the meek would be obliged to move into the parsonage woodshed.

Miss Fesant's school concerts came as manna to the poor, if not the meek. They did not approve dancing any more than the others, but it was something new to the Siding—and it was free. They crowded the little schoolhouse to the doors to watch their offspring clodhopping about the floor. Under this stimulus the concerts became frequent. More, Miss Fesant began to make personal appearances. Not in the cherished ballet costume of course—such a display of her unsuspected limbs would have been misunderstood at Duffy's Siding. But in the Isadora Duncan manner she hovered in the background in flowing draperies and interpreted the Spirit of Spring and other themes while her pupils performed. It was received as something vaguely uplifting if slightly unbecoming in a female of Miss Fesant's position. But it left Miss Fesant unsatisfied.

The spirit of Terpsichore, which had refused to be cribbed within the walls of a boardinghouse bedroom, was cabined and confined now in this schoolhouse full of doubting parents. Terpsichore had led Miss Fesant far from her old shrinking self. It was not that she wanted to display her lissom figure and her really charming legs. She craved the thrill and warmth of footlights, of music, of an audience sensitive to the finer things of life. All these things lay in Cannellton, thirty miles of dirty road away, with a population of two or three thousand and a talking-picture show. Impossible, of course. But was it? She pondered it through many a sleepless night, and at last, after several burning resolves and craven weakenings, she went to Cannellton in Willie Blore's car, along with His Majesty's mails, and sought out the proprietor of the show. Cannelton was known to motion-picture salesmen as a punk show town, a Saturday-night town in the sticks. For this reason Mr. J. Shelley Ditmars operated as his chief line of business a fruit-and-candy store, with ice-cream parlor attached.

Mr. Ditmars received Miss Fesant with a rather anxious smile, a worried hospitality, suspecting that the local Council of Women had sent a delegate to object to "Furnace Love," the coming feature at his Opera House. Under the inquisitive noses of Cannellton candy shoppers he swept her out of the store and into his office. When she blurted out her mission he was astonished.

"A hoofin' act! I dunno, Miss—Miss—"

"Caroline Fesant."

"Miss Pheasant, I don't know what to say. The talkies've put that kind o' thing out o' business. A few show people drift up this way doin' one-night stands but—I'll be frank with you Miss Partridge—they're poor stuff. Burlesque show here five or six months ago—outfit from Toronto, or so they said. Terrible. Show flopped right here. Manager lit out. Had to ship 'em out o' town myself to get 'em off my hands."

"But I'm not a burlesque show," Miss Feasant said with dignity. "I am"—her lips fluttered over the splendid word—"a danseuse, Mr. Ditmars."

Mr. Ditmars thought she looked more like a backwoods school-ma'am, but he did not like to say so. He was a round little man of fifty, with pippin cheeks and sandy hair that was getting a bit sparse on top. In his youth he had married a doll-faced creature who turned out to have little more than the face and a temper, not even, as Mr. Ditmars sometimes sighed to himself, a "figger." He had been a thankful widower for fifteen years, with no more illusions about women. He had none about Miss Fesant. He broke it to her gently.

"I—ah—I can't afford it, Miss. That's a fact."

Miss Fesant made her eyes very large. "But it won't cost you a cent, Mr. Ditmars. I'm not a professional"—how glibly that word came!—"I dance, Mr. Ditmars, for the simple love of it."

"You mean—it's free?" Mr. Ditmars had never heard of such a thing.

Mr. Ditmars," she begged, "let me go on your stage—for once, for five minutes—between the pictures. Then you'll see. And if the audience likes me, perhaps I'll come again. But I don't want any money."

Mr. Ditmars searched for another weapon. "Pianna!" he ejaculated. "Pianna's out o' tune—full o'moths, y'know—all that. Besides, it'd cost a dollar to hire a pianna-player."

"I'll gladly pay for the tuning, and for the pianist," said the danseuse loftily.

The last of his defenses was gone. He could not say a blunt No, not under the gaze of those enormous grey eyes. He was bewildered. He looked at the cheap jacket and the long out-of-date skirt and thought she was a little mad. He saw the queer passion in her eyes and was sure of it. But he could not say No. After all, she might put on a good act, and the Cannellton *Courier* would commend him for his enterprise, as if he had paid for it. Mr. Ditmars spoke his thought aloud.

"What have I got to lose?" asked Mr. Ditmars of the gods.

"What indeed," said Miss Fesant.

"I'll do it, Miss—er—Pigeon. I'll give you a spot—let me see, dark house Monday, Wednesday and Friday, see?—give you a spot Tuesday night between Mickey Mouse and the feature. Be here eight o'clock sharp, see? If you don't mind my sayin' so, it seems a bit queer, but I'll try anything once. What'll I announce?"

Miss Fesant stilled the song in her heart for a moment. "Just put on the screen, 'Caroline Fesant, Danseuse.' No — wait a moment. Make it 'Caro — Caro Fesant, Danseuse.' "

"Carrow Pheasant Dancers," repeated Mr. Ditmars, busy with a pencil.

The Opera house was a long shingled box near the end of Main Street. The flat roof had a wooden parapet with embrasures to suggest castellated walls, and a ventilating cupola, white with pigeon droppings, rose from the midst of it like a donjon keep that had shrunk in the sun. The side and rear walls were unpainted and afflicted with mange where patches of old shingles had curled away and dropped to the ground. But the front was a staring eye-smiting blue, with a large electric sign. A flight of wooden steps, wide at the bottom and narrowing swiftly, led the eye and the customers toward the big red doorway and the little ticket booth where, thrice a week, J. Shelley Ditmars sat with his ticket roll and neat little columns of change.

She inspected the interior in mingled fear and triumph. It was a dismal place. With the advent of talking pictures the old stage had been cut back hopefully to make room for more seats, leaving a twelve-foot space before the big white screen. From that space orators harangued Cannellton audiences at election time, perched like large and noisy sparrows on a window ledge. There were footlights, a miracle. The sockets were empty. She would have to speak to Mr. Ditmars about that. She stood for a full minute gazing over the dim rows of empty seats, populating them with the citizenry of Cannellton, hearing thunders of applause from the red plush thirty-five-cent rows and approving whistles from the gallery, where the projection box reared its white asbestos walls.

She turned, a little dizzy with exaltation, and found herself in the murky backstage. At one time there had been two dressing rooms, male and female. These had been robbed of all privacy to make space for the battery of loudspeakers and other equipment which lurked behind the screen. In a naked place marked "Ladies Dressing" a rickety chair stood mournfully before the cracked grey ghost of a mirror. Three or four dingy powder puffs littered the dressing table, relics of the last stand, with a saucer full of cigarette butts, dry and dusty and faintly stained with lip-rouge. The soiled plaster walls bore many inscriptions, with dates going back an incredible time. The most recent, done with lipstick, contained nine exotic feminine names in a crimson loop, and below, "Stuck in the sticks. Oh you Toronto." A single unclean window looked down upon a hollow filled with the rusty bones of dead automobiles, and a swamp beyond. In its mutilation, its draughts and darkness, its dust that lay thick like a sediment from that darkness, the backstage of Ditmars' Opera House bore witness to the death of vaudeville and the light of other days.

It should have discouraged Caro Fesant, Danseuse. Instead, it sent her briskly forth to buy two or three light bulbs and to hunt up a pianist. She must have a rehearsal now, there would be no other chance. Foreseeing the need, she had brought with her a woollen jumper and a pair of cotton slacks, together with her dancing shoes. Into these she changed, in the dusty Ladies Dressing, while the pianist wakened tinny echoes with an instrument long resigned unto death.

There is little to say of that rehearsal. It was Miss Fesant's first attempt at the ballet in anything larger than a bedroom, and the pianist's first excursion into the higher forms of dance music. Miss Fesant went back to Duffy's Siding in a state of delighted exhaustion. The pianist, a tall hollow-faced young man in horn-rimmed glasses, went straight to the Government liquor store and then retired from the world and its perplexities for twenty-four straight hours.

On Tuesday Miss Fesant conducted her school in a misty dream, and at closing time she flew to the Widow Anderson's, to her room; to the bed where she had communed so often with her soul. At supper time she was still there. She did not want food, she said. The Widow Anderson was concerned. She tried the door. It was not locked. She went in.

"Caroline," said Mrs. Anderson, "whatever is the matter? Are you sick?"

Miss Fesant sat up on the bed. Her big grey eyes shone feverishly. They lit her pale face like lamps.

"Mrs. Anderson, I-I'm dancing—tonight—on a real stage."

"Well," said the widow sensibly, "that's nothing to starve yourself about."

"Oh—but it's the Opera House stage—you know, in Cannellton."

There was a silence. Their eyes talked, Miss Fesant's defiant, the widow's dismayed.

"You're goin' to dance," said the widow faintly, "in—in the rig you showed me that night—them little doll-skirts and the long white stockin's?"

"Yes."

Again the silence. Mrs. Anderson sat beside her. "Caroline, have you figgered it all out, my dear? I'm not one o' these Siding people, thank the good Lord, but I marrit a Siding man and here I am, for better or for worse. I know 'em, my dear. They've stood for your dancin' notions because they can't be choosy 'bout teachers on the money they pay. But, I tell you, my dear, they won't stand for this. It's only thirty miles, after all; and half the Siding women's got relations in Cannellton."

"Yes. Yes, I know."

"Showin' yourself before men folk, I mean, in a get-up like that. I used to hear 'em talk about the vodyvill women that come to Shelley Ditmars' theayter."

"I know. But this is different. This is art."

Miss Fesant saw herself leaping from those shabby shadows at the Opera House, flashing like a tall white moth in the footlights, defying her background and the law of gravity and the birth date on her teaching license in one epochal performance.

"Art," said the Widow Anderson hopelessly.

She hired Willie Blore to drive her to Cannellton. Knowing that only a very great urgency could have induced her to hire him for a special evening trip—"ten cents a mile, fi' dollars for the round trip, seein' it's you"—and seeing the queer exalted look on her face, he tried to draw the reason; but she told him nothing. Only Miss Fesant's slim tense body bumped and swayed beside Willie over the dreary miles to Cannellton. Her spirit was already on the stage. And her body with instinctive cunning left Willie's car at the wrong end of Main Street, telling him to wait outside the Victoria Hotel, and slipped through a back lane to the stage door of the Opera House. There was J. Shelley Ditmars, a worried man. He had done the honors faithfully, haunted by the queer appeal in her eyes, with posters—at two dollars a dozen

from the Cannellton Courier Printer—all over Main Street and in the
windows of outlying stores, declaring Caro Fesant Danseuse a special
attraction, for Tuesday night only.

"Phew!" breathed Mr. Ditmars. "Thought you'd got scared and
changed your mind."

"I'm scared," admitted the strange Miss Fesant gaily, "but all I'm
going to change is my clothes." She was amazed at her own
insouciance.

A single bulb glowed in the lonely Ladies Dressing, hanging from
the eternal darkness of the rafters by a thread, like an incandescent
spider.

Thoughtful Mr. Ditmars had tacked an old picture poster over the
window to shield Miss Feasant's toilette from the junk heap and the
frogs in the swamp. Upon the poster a young woman, frugally-clad,
kicked a contemptuous toe toward Miss Fesant and the canvas backdrop of the talking screen. There was something significant about that.
Beyond the screen was a recurrent buzz of voices, a thudding of seats
flung down in little sporadic bursts like fitful musketry. Mr. Ditmars
could have interpreted that sound very accurately for her. It meant that
Cannellton was entering in small scattered groups, it meant the usual
meagre house of Tuesday night, it cried aloud that Caro Feasant,
Danseuse, meant nothing at all to Cannellton.

The danseuse surveyed herself in the murky glass. As always, the
scanty costume gave her a marvellous feeling of sublimation, as if she
could leap off the earth and remain in suspension indefinitely. She
pirouetted once or twice, flitted up and down the Ladies Dressing on
tiptoe, placed a foot against the grubby wall and threw her torso
backward in the fashion approved by the book. The screen came to life
shockingly, with a blare of strident music followed by voices bellowing
in barrels. It was a weird sensation, for she could see nothing, but she
guessed it was the trailer for Thursday's show. When it ended she heard
a discreet cough from the shadows of the wings and turned to face her
pianist, more goggle-eyed than ever and smelling strongly of whiskey.

"All set, Miss Fesant?"

"Yes. it isn't time yet, is it?"

"In a few minutes." The screen was blaring again. From the
wings she had a distorted view of the screen, enormous figures capering
and squawking; she was filled with contempt for them. She waited,

with a thumping heart, but confident. Suddenly the thing came to an end with a final blast of music from the screen, a final chuckle from the darkness. The footlights sprang up, an upheaval of blinding light with the force of an explosion, and somewhere beyond, the tinkle of a piano. From the gloomy wings Caro Fesant leaped forth, with outflung undulating arms.

Shelley Ditmars had borrowed and placed at each end of the narrow stage a fern in a tall basket-work stand, to soften the barrenness. Miss Fesant sprang into a white blindness, cannoned heavily into the right-wing fern, and sent it crashing into the little pit where her pianist valiantly hammered the "Dance of the Swan." His music ceased abruptly, and in the stark silence, in the blaze of Shelley Ditmars' footlights, Caro Fesant performed a series of staggering bounds, carried forward by her own impetus, struggling desperately for balance. She managed it just short—precariously short—of the fern at the other end. The audience came out of its blank astonishment. Laughter ran over the Tuesday night house like the thin splash of a little sea on a pebble beach. There were whistles from the twenty-centers in the gallery. The pianist recovered himself at about the same time. He began again. Caro Fesant leaped at unseen daffodils, plucked them, tossed them in air. All her long training, the patient back-bendings, the torturing toe-exercises, the book-swayings and book-posturings came into play. Those who hold that dancers are born, not made, should have seen Miss Fesant then. When a sense of rhythm, an iron self-discipline and a single passion are wrapped up in a naturally-flexible body, even a woman past thirty can achieve miracles. For a minute the Tuesday night audience beheld dancing as good as anything they had seen, and began to wonder if it was a comedy act, after all. This Miss Fesant reassured them.

Bedroom floors had not prepared her for Shelley Ditmars' stage. From a momentary pose near the right wings the boards stretched away like a floodlit street. A long twirling run on her handsome legs began brilliantly. Then came a step too long, a dip that went over too far, and she was sprawling.

Mr. Ditmars made for the gallery stairs and burst into the projection booth like a thrown ball.

"Them footlights! Turn 'em off quick!"

Caro Fesant picked herself up in utter darkness. In the little pool of light over the piano, with the clarity of a flash photograph, she could see the hollow young man staring with glassy eyes into the dark which now enfolded her. Then the spotlight came on, a bleak beam from the projection booth. It was not a proper spotlight. It gave Miss Fesant a blue, unearthly appearance, and the sudden plunge from white blindness to darkness and then to this groping blue finger, which now missed her and now caught up with her, these things completed her discomfiture. The audience gave tongue, a thin exuberant howl. Doggedly the pianist hammered out music. Blindly Miss Fesant danced. The spotlight played tag with her, up and down the narrow stage. In the alternative light and eclipse she tripped and stumbled, and made superb recoveries; she kicked the remaining fern into the audience; she pirouetted, and nearly pitched over the dark footlights.

"Will the curtain work?" hissed Shelley Ditmars.

"No."

"Then turn on the feature, quick!"

The screen sprang into life, leaving the danseuse in a merciful dusk near the end of the stage, and in that dusk she fled, with the opening blast of "Furnace Love" stilling the applause behind her.

Shelley Ditmars made his way backstage cautiously, as if it were a haunted house. Caro Fesant sat in the dismal Ladies Dressing, on the one rickety chair, in the light of the one pale bulb, weeping violently on the dresser top.

"It's only me," Shelley said quietly. "Go ahead and cry."

If Miss Fesant heard, she ignored. She was a pitiful but at the same time a strikingly graceful figure, with her long white-sheathed legs curved to one side and her slim back turned upon Mr. Ditmars. He sat on a fragment of ancient scenery and regarded her with kindly eyes. She looked very lonely and forlorn. He waited and watched, with infinite patience. At last, when he had reached the degree of long silences, broken by occasional quick sniffs, with her face turned sideways, cheek on hands, he spoke.

"Here's a clean hank'chiff. Blow your nose."

She put out a hand for the thing, without lifting her rumpled head.

"It was all my fault," Shelley said. "Them darn ferns."

"It wasn't that," she said.

"No, it was the lights. I wanted to do the thing right, see? I told Bill Tumley to fix up the footlights with bulbs, make sure there was plenty o' light. I should'a checked up on him. He put a hundred-watt bulb in every one o' them sockets."

"I couldn't see," she confessed. "My eyes hurt so. But it was my own fault. You warned me."

"Well, anyway," he said encouragingly, "you got your school."

"I can't go back there."

He nodded slowly. "The audience, Miss Fesant—they like the ack, see? They thought it was a comedy ack. Did you hear 'em clappin'?"

Miss Fesant sat up. She faced him fiercely. Tears had smudged her powder and rouge but she did not care. "I suppose you're going to tell me to go to Hollywood or somewhere and get myself a job as a comic actress!"

He wagged his head slowly. There was a queer shy smile on his round face.

"I was goin' to say," he said, examining his freckled hands with enormous interest, "them people didn't know any better. I was goin' to say I liked it, because I remember a time when dancin' was dancin' and music was music, not this St. Vitus stuff they do nowadays. My father built this theayter. In those days we used to get pretty good shows, 'specially in the summer time, when people come around from the big circuits. Vaudeville was something, then. I used to set out there—we had hard wooden seats them days—watchin' them people on the stage, and worshippin' 'em. I know good dancin' when I see it. Everything went wrong for you tonight, but I know good dancin' when I see it. It takes time, and practice, and your heart in it, to do the steps you was doin'. I'm an old-fashioned man, Miss Fesant, and sentimental. When I saw you tonight it brought back the old times. The old good time that'll never come back again. The world was a kindly place then, and life was gentle and easy-goin' and entertainment wasn't just a high fever set to music. I was goin' to say somethin' else, Miss Fesant, on'y I didn't hardly dare. You're a young woman and I'm a little fat man o'fifty. I was goin' to ask you to marry me."

"But I don't know you!" Miss Fesant cried.

"You see me," he said simply. "All I am is what you see. I got a good business and a white clapboard house on Ellum Street, and I come o' decent people. My mother was a schoolmarm like you, and my father was a Presbyterian elder that could lead in prayer."

Caro Fesant's grey eyes were very wide. She drew her white silk knees together. There were new tears in her eyes. "It's awfully kind of you, Mr. Ditmars. But I—I couldn't."

"And all I'd ask of you," Mr. Ditmars pursued gently, "is this. Once a week, on a Monday night, say, when there's no show, we'd come in here, you and me. We'd lock the doors. I'd get some decent lights for them footlights. I'd get a gramophone with the proper kind o' music. And then you'd dance—just for me. For old time's sake."

The pianist, exploring uncertainly in the backstage darkness, turned the corner of Ladies Dressing just in time to see the danseuse fling herself on her knees before Shelley Ditmars and bury her head in his lap. Mr. Ditmars stroked her hair. "Oh, Mr. Ditmars!" cried Miss Fesant. "Oh, Mr. Ditmars!"

The Miracle

The missing boy was one of a brood who lived in a shack on the skirts of Tropesville. His father was away on the Banks in a fishing schooner and his mother was one of those hopeless, woman-in-the-shoe creatures who produce another child every year for the Ladies' Aid to clothe. The boy was fourteen and someone had lent him an old .22 rifle to hunt rabbits on the barrens west of the town.

He had left home yesterday morning, dressed in his patched blue overalls, a Mackinaw two sizes too large for him, a red wool stocking cap and a pair of lumbermen's rubbers. The woman had given him a hunk of bread and a slice of cheese to put in his pocket for lunch. When he failed to turn up that night she was unworried, thinking he might have decided to sleep at "Uncle Charlie's" or at "my Sister Em's" in the casual fashion of the shack dwellers. But on the following forenoon she came, weeping wildly, to the Mounted Police office in Elm Street, with a child in her arms and four or five more tagging at her heels, announcing that her Jimmy was lost in the woods.

The corporal was away on an assault case at Kelly's Cove, and Constable Cawfield received this woeful deputation alone. He was a wiry young man with stiff sandy hair and an energetic nose. He cursed under his breath and reached at once for his cap and greatcoat. These people who lived on the rocky slope behind Tropesville were always losing track of their young'uns. The little town stretched along a shelf between the woods and the sea, and it seemed to Constable Cawfield that he spent half his time dragging the harbor or beating the blooming bush for kids from the shacks. Still, that was not the point. The point was that this silly woman had let twenty-four hours go by without making the most casual inquiries. He looked at the thermometer outside the police-office window. It said five below zero. Last night it had been much colder than that.

The worst of it was that the woman had no idea where the boy had gone, and behind Tropesville stretched the wooded wilderness of Western Nova Scotia, a very big haystack in which to hunt so small a needle. It was a simple matter to spread the alarm—ten minutes at the telephone and a furious clanging of church bells brought fifty men to the hunt—but time was wasted in empty inquiries before they got a clue. The boy had set out along the shore highway and thumbed a ride on one of the trucks that hauled lumber from the mill at Dutch Cross.

Someone had told him that the rabbits were thick as fleas in the woods by Black River, fifteen miles west of Tropesville, and he had asked the truck driver to let him off there. He would thumb a ride back in the afternoon, he said. The driver had seen the boy walking toward an old tote road that ran up the east bank of Black River, and that was all he knew.

Now the hunt was on. As the cars swung out along the shore road they met the bleak breath of a rising southeast wind. There was no sun. A mat of livid cloud came down to the sea like the backdrop of a stage, and in the foreground a few gulls beat the air forlornly, their wings sharply white against it. The sea was the color of lead and the waves running in toward the road were tipped with white. Between the road and the sea ran a narrow sandy beach where the waves collapsed in yellow foam and balls of the gathered froth came bowling across the road in front of the cars. The road was bare. To the right, the grass of the scattered fields was brown and dead and the marshland was dotted with gray frozen pools. A January thaw had wiped off the snow five days ago, filling every stream to a black torrent. Then the weather had turned iron-hard. There had been three days of subzero weather. At Tropesville the lumbermen were praying for snow and it looked as if their prayers might be answered mighty soon. Snow was written all over that hard sky. The wind from the sea howled the very word: Sno-o-o-o-o-ow!

There was not much talk in the police car. Cawfield wore his fur cap and blue topcoat, but he had put off the high brown-polished boots for a pair of moccasins and two pairs of heavy country-wool socks, gartered below the knees of his breeches with a strand of bright green yarn. The other men had a variety of winter clothing—moccasins, lumbermen's rubbers, shoepacks, breeches or long frieze trousers, leather coats, windbreakers and Mackinaws, and all sorts of hats and caps. Cawfield's passengers included Belden, the lumber merchant, Jarvis, the garage proprietor, and Phalen, the schoolmaster. These three had hunted and fished a good deal together and were pretty much at home in the woods. The fourth passenger was the Reverend Porteous, who had never been in the woods, except on summer picnics. The things he wore were mostly borrowed and were either too large or too small for him. On his guant head was a green wool skating cap of his daughter's. It would be warmer than a hat, she said, and he could pull it down over his ears when he got out of the car.

There were ten or twelve cars in the party, all traveling fast. They swept through a small fishing hamlet and on past more bleak marsh-land dotted with brown clumps of rhododendron bushes and twiggy spires of hackmatack. The road climbed a long hill and turned away from the sea a little, with woods on both sides swishing and swaying in the wind. After three or four miles of this, the road dropped again and they came to a small river tumbling toward the sea through a shallow rock gorge and spanned by a black iron bridge. Beyond the bridge the road went up a long hill in carefully graded steps.

The cars stopped at the bridge and turned off the highway into a clearing by the river. There was a mound of sawdust, gray with weather and frozen hard. Bits of rotten edgings and slabs stuck out of it like bones. Beside it tottered the ruin of a sawmill.

The men jumped from the cars briskly and there was a loud slamming of doors. They were representative of Tropesville: fishermen, lumbermen, some hands from Belden's woodworking plant, an assortment of workmen and store clerks.

They crowded around Constable Cawfield and he looked them over shrewdly. He knew most of them. They knew how to get around in the woods. He asked about compasses and was relieved to find that everyone, except Mr. Porteous, had one.

There was a recognized technique for hunting lost kids in the woods around Tropesville. The searchers simply formed a sort of skirmish line and then advanced through the suspected area, making all the noise possible. The fishermen had brought along their tin dory horns, several men had shotguns, and two members of the Tropesville band had brought along their gleaming brass cornets.

Cawfield had strong doubts about this method. Apart from the fact that a lost kid might be scared and hide at the approach of such weird sounds, there was the point that a man walking through the woods blowing a horn might be nothing but a confusing will-o'-the-wisp to a lost soul in the distance. But Cawfield said nothing. He had served for a time in the north. He had a strong notion that it was going to snow before long, and the horns would be useful in keeping the searchers in touch with one another.

He pulled out a map and spread it on the frozen crust of the sawdust pile. It was a soiled sheet badly worn at the folds, a relic of bygone logging operations on Black River. The stream wandered down the central fold and on both sides there were jumbled squares and rectangles in faded red ink marking the boundaries of timber lots cut and forgotten years ago. East of the river the land sloped to an irregular ridge three or four miles from the stream, and beyond that was a featureless country of rocky ridges and swampy intervales. In time the uplands had covered with scrub hardwood, and now there was a tangle of wire birch, maple, oak and poplar fifteen to twenty feet high. In it there was no field of view except from a treetop on one of the ridges, and then nothing to see but a bristle of thick winter-bare bush in which an army might have stood concealed. The uplands, too, were veined with faint paths kept open by moose and deer, all that was left of the old logging roads, a maze in which the lost boy might wander for weeks if he lived so long. Halfway up the map, the river forked. The main branch wriggled off to the northwest; the lesser branch came in from the northeast and east, and Constable Cawfield put a square-nailed finger on it.

"Mr. Belden, I wish you'd take a half dozen men and push straight up the tote road to the fork—it's about six miles—and see if you can find any sign of the kid crossing the east branch on the ice. I've got a hunch he followed the first ridge pretty well after he left the tote road, and if he kept going he'd come to that side of the fork."

"But then he'd have sense enough to follow the river down," Beldon objected.

"You never know what a kid's going to do. 'Course, I'm hoping to find him somewhere in the uplands east of the river here. It's the only hope. We've only got five hours or so of daylight and it'll be snowing by dark."

The men nodded and grunted. The boy had been thirty hours or more in the bitter cold; no doubt he had kept moving to save himself from freezing, but he must be very tired. The snowstorm tonight would finish him.

Belden and his party moved off.

"The rest of us," Cawfield said crisply, "will start up the tote road behind Belden. It follows the east bank up to the fork, with old log hauls running off the right every few hundred yards. I want a man to strike up each of those log hauls as we come to 'em. Follow 'em back into the country five or six miles, then turn north or south, whichever you like—parallel to the river anyhow—for a mile or so, and finally head back towards the tote road and the river. You should all be back at the river by dark."

"Why?" Mr. Porteous asked.

"Because you can't move in the woods after dark, sir. Besides, there's a storm coming up. I don't want this business gummed up by some of the searching party getting lost. That's happened to me before and I got h..., I got ticked off by division for it."

The tote road was six feet wide and sunk a foot or so below the level of the forest floor.

It was like a stream bed with its stones and frozen puddles. The stones bore old scars of sleds and wagon wheels. To the left the river gleamed through a fringe of firs and alders. This stretch below the fork was too rapid to freeze, even in the coldest weather.

As the troop moved off, the fishermen began to blow their horns as if they were adrift in their dories in a Bank fog, a ragged chorus of queer calf blattings that reminded Cawfield of Montreal on New Year's Eve. The members of the town band took off their mittens and fingered their instruments as they tramped along.

One said uncertainly, "Spose we might's well play a tune as just blow." The other nodded. There was some hesitation and then, with a glance toward the Reverend Porteous, they struck up Onward, Christian Soldiers. Added to the blatting of the dory horns and the shocking boom-boom of shotguns, it made sound enough, in the three-walled confines of the tote road anyhow, to wake the dead. Cawfield thought whimsically, *All we need now is a tambourine for the collection.* He was not a religious man, though he saw the importance of someone being earnest in a naughty world. He approved of the church as a pillar to the law, but rested his own faith in the law—and himself.

A gap appeared in the trees to the right, one of the old log hauls coming down to the river, half choked with huckleberry bushes and second-growth spruce and fir. One man dropped out and followed it up the slope. The rest moved on quickly, turning down their Mackinaw collars. The raw sea wind could not reach them here in this narrow slot in the bush, but overhead the treetops hissed like the sea itself. At intervals a log haul opened to the right and a man turned off, visible for twenty feet or so before the bush swallowed him. The orchestra dwindled, and as each musician dropped out and disappeared, the rest could hear his horn, faintly for a few steps and then not at all. The wind had shifted to the east and carried these petty sounds across the river.

At last Cawfield and the preacher were alone. The policeman had purposely kept Mr. Porteous beside him, and now he said, "Well, here's another log haul and here we go."

The Reverend Porteous protested, "Let me go up here and you take the next. We'll cover that much more ground, won't we?"

"We'll stick together," said Cawfield, knowing very well that Mr. Porteous, alone, would get lost in twenty minutes. But seeing the stubborn set of the old man's jaw, he added craftily, "You see, we're the farthest upriver—barring Belden's lot, who've gone straight to the fork—and spose we find the kid? Spose he's too weak to walk, eh?

Down, maybe. Feet frozen—anything. One man couldn't carry him far—a big kid like that. But two of us—"

"Ah!" breathed Mr. Porteous. "Lead on! Lead on!"

Last week's thaw had made bad footing where the trail grew steep. The rain and melting snow had poured down the slope and then frozen in little cascades of ice. The ground under the trees was bare, except in the hollows, where the shrunken remains of snowdrifts lay gray and soiled, like discarded bread crusts, amongst the brown dead leaves. The ferns were bent and broken by the weight of the snow that had come and gone, and their brown fronds rustled against the men's boots in a harsh continuous whisper. All the big hardwoods were bare. The young maples were bare. But here and there a few dead leaves clung stubbornly to a small oak or beech, clashing and rattling in the wind, a desolate sound.

Mr. Porteous wondered sometimes if the path were not a mere game track, but he was reassured when his plunging feet struck bits of corduroy in the hollows, rotten poles drooping between the moldered brown lengths of the stringpieces, all hidden in the undergrowth. Cawfield explained these things over his shoulder as he went along, and pointed out the bends in the track where the bygone loggers had swerved to avoid a big boulder or a hole.

The policeman set a stiff pace, anxious to make the most of the daylight. The Reverend Porteous had seldom been in the woods—never in winter—but his long legs and bony frame seemed quite adapted to this sort of thing and he felt rather pleased with himself. His daughter had objected to his going, but he was only fifty-six and had always lived abstemiously; a lean horse for a long race, he always said.

In the hollows were many tracks of deer and occasionally moose, made during the thaw and preserved in the frozen mud. It was useless to look for the boy's track in the hard cast, of course, but wherever a scrap of the old snow lay in the path Cawfield examined it with care. The stuff was brittle and dark with specks of bark and lichen from the surrounding trees. It broke underfoot and fell away in shapeless lumps, but again and again Cawfield stooped and satisfied himself before passing over it. Once or twice a rabbit broke cover almost under their feet and raced away up the ridge in a scurry of dead leaves, its gray-white winter coat very distinct against the brown forest floor. Mr. Porteous pictured the eager boy in hot pursuit, getting farther and farther from the tote road and the river, until he was past hope of finding his way back.

The path ended suddenly in a bushy space amongst tall second-growth hemlocks.

"Humph!" said Cawfield. "No more road. The old-timers skidded their logs here and piled 'em for the sled teams hauling down to the river."

Mr. Porteous nodded vaguely. He was warm and the moisture from his hot face condensed on the cold lenses of his glasses. He took them off and wiped them with is handkerchief.

The policemen struck off again toward the east. On the top of the ridge in a little gap in the forest he paused and tipped his face to the sky.

"Snow!" he said.

It was snow, all right, the first hard specks of an old-fashioned January blizzard, if the signs meant anything. He increased his pace eastward and in half an hour they found themselves going downhill through a mixed growth of hardwoods and small spruce and fir. They came to a ravine whose floor bristled with hackmatack trees. They looked dead with their bare crooked limbs and warty twigs, and Mr. Porteous thought how strange it was that a conifer should shed its needles every fall. The ravine had flooded in the thaw and frozen, and afterward the water had drained away and left a shell of ice. The two men broke through to their knees and floundered across noisily. As they climbed the other side of the ravine the ground was already white with snow. Their feet left a herringbone of tracks which gave the preacher, looking back, an odd satisfaction. But there was small time for looking back and the snow sifted down remorselessly; the tracks were blurred in a minute and gone in five. The wind worried the treetops savagely. Below, the air was almost motionless. As the snow increased, it whirled down between the trees in choking spirals of white dust. It gathered along the branches like strips of cotton wool, and whenever the trees suffered a convulsion in the wind the cold stuff dropped on the travelers in crumbling white ropes.

Cawfield, picking a way through the dry mist, had to consult his compass every thirty steps. He held toward the east steadily, but with a growing feeling of hopelessness. The watershed was a jumble of ridges and swales and some of the streams wandered out to the little Muskrat River in the wilderness eastward, a nightmare region of thickets and huge boulders, a byword amongst the older lumbermen. He looked at his watch from time to time, and at four o'clock he stopped with an air of finality. The daylight was fading. There was an ominous dusk already in the softwood clumps. He reckoned his distance from Black River at five, perhaps six miles. There was barely time to get back to the tote road. It would be hard going as the dark increased.

But Mr. Porteous cried sharply, "Don't turn back, constable! Think! The boy may be just another hundred steps ahead!"

Cawfield's snow-crusted fur cap wagged angrily. "Why not to the right? Or the left? Listen, sir! We'll swing a bit south, a mile perhaps. Then west as hard as we can go. We'll have some scrambling in the dark towards the last, as it is."

"No, no! We must go on, I tell you!"

"We're just as apt to find him that way as floundering down into the Muskrat country and spending a useless night in the woods."

"Ah, but how can we go home, to suppers and warm beds, with that poor boy still in the woods? Let us stay the night—make a fire in the shelter of a thicket—and be ready to go on at daylight! After all, constable, we are grown men, warmly clad, and you—I've heard you spent some time in the north—you must have spent more than one night in the snow."

It was on the tip of Cawfield's tongue to say that grown men in the north didn't let themselves get caught in blizzards without ax or snowshoes. His experience and his common sense told him that the preacher's notion was fantastic. Without an ax it was impossible to make any kind of shelter or to get enough firewood to last the night. He did not care about himself; he was tough, he could stick it out. But he had noticed Mr. Porteous breathing harder and shorter for the last two miles. He admired the spirit, but he suspected the good man's flesh. Mr. Porteous' knowledge of the outdoors was confined to some vague memories of the Boy Scout Handbook. Mr. Porteous wouldn't understand that you can't keep moving in the woods in a storm, once darkness falls. Nor would he realize that a man in sweat-soaked underwear can't sit down in a thicket for twelve hours in a zero temperature and live to see the morning.

And what good would any of this do the lost boy? They would be tired in the morning, assuming that they lived through the night, and tired men floundering through the drifts could accomplish nothing.

Better to go home, eat, rest, and return at daylight with snowshoes for a final try. The shore highway was scoured by the full sweep of the wind and was always passable for cars as far as Black River.

"Look here," he said roughly. "You don't know what you're talking about and we're wasting daylight."

"No!" Mr. Porteous said stubbornly.

They faced each other like a pair of snow men, white from head to foot, each face a moist pink blur.

The preacher put his mittened hands to his mouth and shouted hoarsely, "Jimmy! Hi! Jimmy!"

Mr. Porteous had a powerful voice, renowned in Tropesville, but here, walled in by the trees, absorbed by the eddying white mists, defied by the shriek of the wind and the swish of the treetops, it was lifeless.

The preacher listened intently. "Constable! A cry! Didn't you hear a cry over there?" He gestured toward the east, into the teeth of the storm.

"Branches rubbing together, sir. They make all kinds of sounds."

"Ah, but this was a voice, constable! I'm sure of it!" He shouted again, and for better hearing dragged off the snow-crusted skating cap. His long hair—he was rather vain about his fine gray locks and never let the barber clip them higher than his collar—was all tousled by the drag of the tight woolen hat, and now it was matted with snow in a moment.

Cawfield listened tolerantly. He admired his own patience. The storm had filled the woods with voices. If you turned your imagination loose you could hear a cry, a laugh, the Anvil Chorus—anything you chose.

He looked at the preacher again. Mr. Porteous was standing with his face upturned, his mittened hands clasping the shapeless cap against the breast of his borrowed Mackinaw. He was praying. Cawfield was shocked. This kind of thing was all right in a pulpit, but here it was somehow indecent and even weird.

At last Mr. Porteous' lips ceased moving. He took off his glasses and wiped them, blinking severely at the policeman.

"Constable, more things are wrought by prayer than this world dreams of. I tell you I heard a cry—in line with that tree ahead of us. I know the boy is there—somewhere in that direction—as sure as I know there's a heaven above. I am going that way until I find him. You can do what you like—go back to the river if you wish. I absolve you. A cry, you understand. I must go." He pulled on the cap.

Cawfield was appalled at the determination in his gaunt face. "Look here," the policeman said. "If you're bound to go on, I'm bound to go with you. Let me take a compass bearing on that tree."

They plunged off into the storm, Cawfield ahead.

Every hundred steps Mr. Porteous shouted, "Jimmy! Jimmy!" He counted the steps aloud. Once he said, "Why don't you shout, too, constable?"

Cawfield held his tongue. The man was as mad as a hatter. Not real loony, perhaps, but touched in the belfry somewhere. Mr. Porteous strode on behind, lifting his voice to the storm, a stubborn man riding a religious conviction.

"Are we still on course?"

Cawfield examined the compass. "Yes."

"Good! Keep on! Watch the compass carefully, constable. If it wasn't the boy's voice, it was a sign from heaven itself. Faith, constable, faith! There is a faith that can move mountains; surely it can find one of God's creatures in this storm."

They worked across a steep shoulder covered with tall hemlock and spruce. In the shelter of the big snow-laden trees there was pitch darkness. Coming down the far slope they emerged upon a sudden tangle of fallen trees. A trick of the autumn gales had played havoc here, uprooting big maples and birches.

Cawfield made casts to right and left, seeking a way around, but there was none to be seen. He forced a slow and painful way forward, climbing over the dead trunks and clawing desperately through the tangled fir tops and roots. The preacher's breath was whistling through his teeth. Cawfield could hear it as his back above the sounds of the storm. He plunged on ruthlessly.

Suddenly, astonishingly, with all the simple completeness of a good conjuring trick, there was the missing boy! He was immediately before them, crouching in a sort of cave formed by the upturned roots of a fallen maple.

"Hello," said the boy.

Cawfield stood still. He gaped. But Mr. Porteous rushed forward and fell on his knees in the snow, clutching at the boy and crying thanks to the Lord.

The boy drew back, frightened, and said in a thin voice, "I want to go home."

"You all right, son?" Cawfield said. These shack kids were tough.

"Yes, sir. I got lost, huntin' rabbits."

"I know," Cawfield grunted. "Feet all right? Hands? Can you walk?"

"Sure," said the boy, and looked curiously at Mr. Porteous. Mr. Porteous was still giving thanks to God in a voice that carried above the howl of the storm. The boy came out of the cave. "I lost my gun too," he said plaintively. "I kep' walkin' all the time to keep warm. There was a moon last night. I figgered to hole up here till the storm was over. What is the matter with this man?"—indicating Mr. Porteous with a jerk of his ragged stocking cap.

"If you can walk," Constable Cawfield said, "we'll try to make Black River."

"But do you think we can?" asked Mr. Porteous, scrambling to his feet. "We've travelled a long way from it, and it's nearly dark."

Cawfield was tempted to say something about faith, but he murmured simply, "We can try, sir, anyhow."

The policeman led off, with the boy next, and Mr. Porteous brought up the rear. Mr. Porteous kept up, with a breathless sort of heartiness, a flow of encouraging remarks to the boy. The boy said very little. Cawfield said nothing at all.

They worked out of that maze of windfalls and plunged into a stand of big hemlocks where the darkness was total. The dense crowns of these trees had shut out most of the snow, there was not enough to cover the projecting roots; the men and the boy kept stubbing their toes and slithering and falling. At short intervals Cawfield had to stop and consult his compass, blessing the luminous northpointer on the disk. It was a queer game of blindman's buff, with the boy clutching Cawfield's coat and the preacher clutching the boy's Mackinaw belt.

After what seemed an age they worked out of the big trees and found themselves struggling downhill in thickets of young spruce and fir, a veritable forest of Christmas trees without ornament and set down much too close together. The snow was drifted deeply amongst them and it weighed down the branches so that the travellers had to paw them aside with swimming gestures; they choked and spluttered as if drowning in this confused white sea. The exertion was terrific.

Cawfield wondered if the boy could hold out. He was beginning to feel the strain himself. He had ordered each of them to hang on to the coattail in front for the sake of keeping together, but their tendency was to drag more and more, and he had become a sort of human locomotive pulling the whole blind train.

"Have to stop!" gasped Mr. Porteous. "Just a minute! Get my breath!" They stopped, half squatting, half sitting in the snow, while the sweat on their skins turned cold and the wind seemed to blow along their naked spines.

Soon—too soon—Mr. Porteous arose and said he could go on. In twenty minutes he was begging for breath again.

This time they rested ten minutes and the cold began to search their bodies in earnest.

"How far is it, constable, do you think?" the preacher asked.

"Oh, not far. We can make it. We've got to! Let's get going!"

Cawfield ceased pulling the branches aside now and threw his weight against them, shouldering them apart. Unexpected yieldings sent him sprawling. Whenever this happened, Mr. Porteous and the boy came down upon him headlong. They rolled, blind and stifled, pawing at one another in the smother, like drunks in a gutter.

In one of these affairs Cawfield dropped the compass and they spent an age on hands and knees groping desperately in the snow before they found it. In another, Mr. Porteous lost his glasses, but the policeman would not stop for those.

At last the constable burst through a mass of snowy branches and fell on his face in a narrow place where the snow flew like rock salt blown from a gun. As he raised himself he felt something under his hands—the hard spatulate clods left in the snow by tramping boots not long before.

"Why," he said, "it must be—"

There was a lull in the wind and they heard the river roaring. They were kneeling in the tote road.

The cars, snow-plastered, looked like igloos in the clearing at the bridge. As the three figures stumbled out of the tote road, somebody switched on his headlights; all the doors seemed to fly open at once, spewing dim forms that came shouting toward them. The headlights made hard white bars in the snowy dark. Men swarmed about them, patting them on the back, making a great fuss over the boy. Someone offered him a vacuum bottle of hot cocoa, which he took cautiously. He seemed quite unconcerned about the whole affair. He wanted to go home, he said. The men cried questions, and Mr. Porteous, blinking owlishly, declared that Constable Cawfield must tell the story of the finding of the boy. Mr. Porteous was filled with a quite understandable triumph. He had clung to faith, over Cawfield's skepticism and worldly wisdom, and his faith had won. It had been a terrible journey and he would never forget it as long as he lived.

"Tell them, constable!" he urged. "Tell them the simple truth!"

Constable Cawfield sucked hard on the cigarette that someone had put in his mouth. The truth? He was tempted. The truth was that he had made up his mind to get Mr. Porteous out of the woods, by hook or by crook, from the moment the man began to hear voices, back there in the ridges. After they set off in pursuit of the preacher's obsession, Cawfield had gradually and cunningly shifted the course from east to south, and then from south to west—in fact, all the time that Mr. Porteous thought they were plunging into the Muskrat wilderness, they were, in fact, going all-out for the Black River tote road. Cawfield had felt a little guilty at first, but he had seen men go queer in storms up north and he was taking no chances with Mr. Porteous. They had stumbled on the boy not more than two miles from the tote road. But those two miles had been terrible—it had taken an hour to make the last few hundred yards—Mr. Porteous believed he had traveled a great distance. Cawfield was tired and his short temper was on edge. He had a mind to tell the truth in quick phrases that were on the tip of his tongue. But he paused, licking his cracked lips. After all, it had been remarkable, stumbling on the boy in that unlikely fashion. It was quite wonderful, any way you looked at it—a miracle, you might say.

He said it. "It was a miracle."

Mr. Porteous beamed.